SIDELINES

PART THIRTEEN

J Ware

ISBN-13: 978-1-950650-45-3

COMING SOON,

J WARE'S

6TH SERIES,

"TwinInsanity"

Prologue

Two weeks later…

Everyone was in the backyard at Lillian's home for her and Lawrence's wedding. It was a small ceremony with only family and friends. Shavon, Valerie, and Jaeda were in the house and upstairs in one of the bedrooms.

Valerie was sitting on the bed, while Jaeda was sitting on the couch; Shavon was standing and shaking her head. Valerie slightly laughed. "Does anybody else think us being Miss Brooks' bridesmaids is inappropriate?" Jaeda looked at her and then slightly laughed, as Shavon rolled her eyes. "Uh yeah, but she asked, so what was I gonna say?" Jaeda frowned, as she looked at Shavon. "Maybe, no…and thanks for answering for me and Val; we really appreciate it." Shavon gave Jaeda a snide look and didn't appreciate her sarcasm. "Whatever, Jaeda…it makes sense, if you think about it; but anyways, at least we got Val back in town for the weekend."

Valerie looked at them and then rolled her eyes. "Uh huh…well, who are the groomsmen?" Shavon looked at Valerie. "Vance, Randy, and Lawrence's sons; he got two sons." The women nodded and then Valerie stood from the bed; Jaeda followed her lead and then cleared her throat. "So, if Vance is in the wedding, then that means, Trisha is here, right?" Shavon looked at Jaeda and then nodded. Valerie looked at Jaeda too and then back to Shavon. "How's it going with that? I mean, I know it has to be weird now, with her married to Vance again…and you being with his brother now." Shavon sighed and understood where the women were going with their line of questioning; it was weird to her and did bother her, but she kept her feelings to herself and played it off.

Shavon shrugged her shoulders. "It's cool…Randy and Vance are close now, and they hang out, but me and Trisha don't. I don't really see her, but I'm not trying to be friends with her no way." Valerie nodded and Jaeda shook her head. "So, you're not even trying to be good with her?" Shavon frowned, as she looked at Jaeda; she shook her head. "No, for what? That's Vance's wife…when she around, I leave or go in another room." Valerie shrugged her shoulders and was going to leave it alone; she didn't live in Houston anymore, so didn't care either way, if that's how Shavon felt. Jaeda nodded and would also leave it alone, but was curious as to how Trisha felt about all of this.

Before another word could be said, there was a knock on the door and someone stuck their head in, to say that it was time. The women turned to the door and then nodded; afterwards, they all walked out the bedroom, to head downstairs.

In the backyard, Trisha was sitting with the twins, while the other guests were seated; Vance, Randy, Lawrence and his sons, were standing up front already and waiting. The music played and everyone turned around to see Valerie walk out, then Shavon, then Jaeda. The men smiled, as they stood up front. Valerie went to stand on the other side of the officiant, and then Shavon did the same; when it was Jaeda's turn, one of Lawrence's sons frowned, as he looked at her. "Jaeda…" She looked at him and so did everyone else; Jaeda stopped walking and then frowned as well. "Daniel…?" Both smiled and forgot where they were; Daniel walked from beside his dad and went to Jaeda, as she went to him. They both hugged, while Valerie and Shavon looked at each other; Vance frowned, as Lawrence called his son's name, but got nowhere.

Daniel and Jaeda pulled back from each other and continued to smile. "What the hell are you doing here, Daniel?" He shook his head, as he spoke. "Me? Lawrence is my dad…what are you doing here?" Lawrence walked to his son and then grabbed him by the shirt to turn him around. "Uh, excuse me, but can I get married?" Daniel cleared his throat and then nodded. "I'm sorry, dad." Daniel looked back at Jaeda and then walked back over to the guys with his dad. Jaeda quickly went to stand with the women; they looked at her and frowned. She cleared her throat and then looked away.

The ceremony continued, as Daniel looked over at Jaeda; Vance looked at Daniel and then frowned again, while not knowing what was going on. Shortly after, Lillian walked down the aisle and everyone turned to look at her. After she reached the front, she smiled at her groom and he smiled back; they stood in front of each other and then the ceremony commenced.

The ceremony was short, and afterwards, the happy couple held hands, as they turned to everyone and were announced, Mr. and Mrs. Lawrence Henderson. Everyone stood and clapped; the couple walked down the aisle, and the groomsmen and bridesmaids followed behind. Everyone then went inside the house for the reception.

Once in the house, the guests congratulated the happy couple. Daniel pushed his new stepbrother, Vance, out the way, and then went over to Jaeda. Vance frowned, as he fell into Randy; both guys turned to see Daniel fly over to Jaeda. Randy looked at Vance and then shook his head. "Does he know her?" Vance looked at Randy. "For his sake, I hope it was mistaken identity." Vance glanced at Daniel and then shook his head, as he walked away to go over to his mama.

Daniel had made it over to Jaeda and then tapped her on the shoulder; she turned around and then smiled, as Valerie and Shavon watched them interact. "Daniel Henderson…long time, no see." Daniel slightly laughed and then nodded. "Jaeda…I can't even believe it's you; so, are you my stepsister now or something?" Jaeda frowned and then shook her head. "Uh no, I'm not Miss Brooks' daughter, just…I know her." Shavon slightly laughed, as Valerie turned her head away.

Daniel nodded. "Ok, well, that's good to know…" He stopped and then stared at her, as she stared back; Shavon discreetly bumped Jaeda and made her speak. "Uh well, yeah, ok then…it was great to see you again." Daniel nodded. "Ok, well maybe we can talk sometimes…go out." Jaeda opened her mouth to speak and then closed it; she looked back at the women, who were staring at her. Jaeda looked back at Daniel and then nodded. "Sure…that sounds good." He nodded and then said he was going to congratulate his dad and Lillian; she nodded and then after he walked away, Shavon turned Jaeda around. "So, you wanna be killed by Joron, right?" Valerie laughed, as Jaeda rolled her eyes. "It's not like that; me and Daniel worked at a restaurant together, when I was in Atlanta…after I went back to Devonte and before I remembered my life with Rendell. He was cool and I hadn't seen him in years. I use to talk to him about everything."

The women looked at each other and then back to Jaeda; Valerie cleared her throat. "Oh wow, well that's great…you let me know how that friendship goes." Shavon slightly laughed, as Jaeda gave Valerie a snide look. "Whatever, Val…" The women all laughed and then started to enjoy the reception.

As everyone was having a good time, Trisha was by herself and watching everyone enjoy themselves. She was sitting down and had the kids with her; she sighed, as she looked around and then stood from the chair, she was sitting in. Trisha picked up Tristan and grabbed Vander's hand; she was about to walk away, when Vance walked over to her. "Hey, are you having a good time?" Trisha looked at him and then cleared her throat. "Actually no, I'm not; I'm leaving with the kids, but you should stay." Vance slightly frowned, as he stared at her. "You're leaving? Why?" Trisha turned her head to the side and then back to Vance. "I don't feel good and it doesn't look I'll be missed anyway, so…" Vance interjected. "Baby, what are you talking about? It's my mama's wedding reception and…" Trisha interjected. "Stay, Vance…but me and the kids are leaving." Before Vance could respond, Trisha walked away with the kids; Vance watched her and then sighed. Afterwards, he went back over to his brother.

Chapter 1

Two months later…

During the course of the two months, more small ceremonies took place, like the courthouse wedding between Jaeda and Joron, and Rydell and Giani.

* * *

Vance was home from work and just entered the house; he called out for Trisha but didn't receive a response. He hung his keys on the wall and then made his way to the living room; once in there, he saw Trisha on the couch, and the twins playing on the playmat. Vance smiled at her. "Hey, baby; you didn't answer when I called you." Trisha turned her head to him and then nodded. "I'm sorry, I was…thinking." Vance slightly nodded his head, as he went over to the twins; he knelt down and then kissed both of them on the forehead. Afterwards, he turned back to Trisha, while still knelt down. "What were you thinking about?" Trisha shrugged her shoulders. "Not much…just life." Vance sighed and then nodded; he stood up from the floor and then walked over to the couch, to sit down next to her. "Ok, well, my brother invited us over to hang out with him and Shavon." Trisha stared at him and then shook her head. "That sounds great…why don't you go, and take the kids? I'll stay home." Trisha stood from the couch and he frowned.

Vance stopped Trisha, before she walked away. "Hey, wait…" Vance stood from the couch and looked at her, as she turned back around to him. "What's wrong? Ever since my mama's wedding, you don't want to go over there or to my brother's house, either. Is there a reason you're avoiding my family?" Trisha stared at him, and then slightly laughed. "Family, huh? I'm not sure what that is anymore, Vance. Your family consists of Shavon, a woman that you cheated on me with, for God knows how long…a woman that is practically your sister-in-law now." Vance sighed and then turned his head to the side, before looking back at her. "I thought we were past this, Trisha. I don't want Shavon, and she and my brother are happy, like I am with you. You're my wife and I love you, so there's no reason to feel some type of way about being around Shavon."

Trisha sarcastically laughed. "Feel some type of way? Well, I hate to remind you, but everyone's been feeling some type of way about me, since we were married the first time. I don't have any friends and the wives of your friends or significant others, are all the ex-sidelines. I don't belong anywhere with you and I don't think I ever did." Trisha didn't realize that she was crying; she quickly wiped her eyes and then Vance stepped closer to her. "Baby, I hear you, but it's what you're not saying that I'm worried about. So, tell me where you're going with this."

Trisha slightly shrugged her shoulders. "I think maybe we moved too fast..." Vance slowly nodded his head. "So, you don't love me anymore?" Trisha sighed. "I didn't say that...I do love you, but..." Vance interjected. "But nothing, Trisha...I..." Trisha interjected. "Fine...I need some air, so can you watch the twins?" Vance stared at her for a few moments and then nodded. Trisha nodded too and then turned around to walk out the living room, as he watched her. Afterwards, Vance sighed and then sat back down on the couch; Vander walked over to him and then Vance picked him up. Vance sat there with his son, and then sighed.

Chapter 2

Trisha left the house and then drove for about twenty minutes; she reached an office building and then parked in the front. Trisha got out her car and then looked around; she walked to the front door and then went inside. She took her shades off and then hurried to the elevator, to get on. After she got off on the right floor, she hurried down the hall and then went to a door. Trisha didn't knock, but instead opened the door. The man inside, turned his head and then slightly frowned. Trisha closed the door behind her, as the man stared at her. "Trisha?" She nodded, as she slowly walked over to him; she stopped and he shook his head, as he eyed her. "Trisha, I haven't seen you in two years…uh, you look great. How are you?"

Trisha turned her head to the side and then back to him; she shrugged her shoulders and then her lips slightly quivered. "Hey, Ryan…uh, Dr. Graham; I was wondering if we could talk." Ryan sighed and then nodded. "If you wanna talk professionally, then you already know you can't talk to me; but if you're looking for a friend, then I'm here." Trisha sighed. "I need to talk to you professionally, again." Ryan gestured with his hand, for her to have a seat on the couch; she nodded and then went to sit down. Ryan went to sit down on the chair across from the couch. "Trisha…I ethically can't talk to you, as a patient anymore, so…" Trisha interjected. "Alright…fine; I'll see someone else." Trisha was about to get up from the couch, when Ryan stopped her. "No…it's fine…stay." Trisha looked at him and then nodded; she slightly looked down and then back up again at him.

Ryan sat back in the chair and then began. "Ok, it's been a little over two years since I saw you…so, tell me what's been going on with you." Trish sarcastically laughed. "Oh, well, me and Vance started dating and then I became pregnant; then he was shot, by his sister, that he was previously having sex with…then I shot her, when she tried to kill me. Now me and Vance are married again with twins…a boy and girl." Ryan stared at her with his mouth agape; he was rendered speechless. He closed his mouth, as she stared at him and waited for him to say something. He cleared his throat and had to think about his words carefully. "I…I don't know how to respond to all that. Trisha, are you serious? You and Vance are back together and married again? Did you say he was having sex with his sister?"

Trisha sighed and then slightly looked down, as Ryan moved from his chair and then over to sit next to her on the couch; he looked out straight and then back to her. "What happened between you and Vance?" Trisha looked at him. "I went to his birthday party to tell him, happy birthday, and say a few words; afterwards, he asked if we could have drinks sometime. I said, yes, and we slowly started dating; after a few months of dating, I became pregnant." Ryan shook his head and then swallowed hard. "I just don't believe this…that man humiliated and embarrassed you, your entire marriage; you cried at every session we had. He made you feel like you were beneath him and not worthy of him or anyone. How could you go back to him?" Trisha slightly nodded her head, as she listened and then swallowed hard. "Are you speaking as my therapist again or a friend, because right now you sound like you're judging me…and not like my therapist?"

Ryan turned his head to the side and then back to her. "Fine…continue." Trisha sighed and then wiped her eyes. "Shavon is with Vance's brother…and him and his brother are close now, so at family gatherings, we are around Shavon and his family. I feel so out of place now, because things have changed, from when we were married the first time. All his friends are no longer with their wives, that used to be my friends; they're married to their former sidelines…the sidelines are the wives now, and I can't help but feel that everyone is laughing at me, like they were before, when I was clueless and Vance was cheating on me. I feel uncomfortable…and I don't have any friends or any family of my own. I just…" Trisha stopped and then shook her head.

Ryan rubbed his hands down his face and then became angry; he abruptly stood from the couch and then looked down at her. "I can't do this…I can't listen to this anymore. This is just one of the damn reasons why I can't be your therapist anymore. I mean, are you serious, Trisha?" She looked up at him, as he continued on his rant. "Not only are you re-married to Vance, but you have to see the woman that he cheated on you with, because she's with your brother-in-law now; he's probably still cheating on you with her, behind your back and his brother's. I mean, this is ridiculous to me; you made so much progress when we parted ways and had a new lease on life. Now you're back crying in my office and depressed again. Make me understand what's going on!" Trisha jumped when he yelled at her; she then stood from the couch and grabbed her purse, so she could leave.

Ryan cursed to himself and then went after her; he caught her at the door and then turned her around to him. "Wait…Trisha, I'm sorry, but please make me understand why." Trisha turned her head to the side and then back to him. "I love him…and I don't think I ever stopped; that will never change, but you are right about everything. I can't help how I feel about him and it seems that he changed, just like I have…we have children now, but I'm not clueless this time around. I just think that we went too fast and I need to do something to slow everything down." Ryan stared at her and then cleared his throat; he nodded. "Come sit back down." Ryan took her hand and then pulled her away from the door, so they could both go sit back down on the couch.

Afterwards, he looked straight. "Trisha, I'm sorry again…not just for everything I just said to you, but for how we ended. I was wrong for my unethical behavior and I never did that before you, during, or after. Me and my wife divorced, not too long after you stopped seeing me." Ryan stopped and then sighed, before he continued. "I'm telling you all this, because I want you to know that I'm here if you need me; if you need a place to go with your children, then you can come stay with me, if you want. This is a conflict of interest for me, but I can't let you speak to another therapist; I'd prefer if you continued seeing me and I promise I won't judge you or speak the way I just did, again." Ryan finally turned his head to Trisha and found her staring at him; she nodded her head. "Ok…"

Ryan nodded and then stood from the couch; he walked over to his desk and then grabbed his prescription pad and pen. Ryan spoke, as he wrote on the pad. "I'm gonna write you a prescription, for your depression. I know it's been a while since you had a prescription for these, but it seems to me that it's time to start you back on them." Ryan tore the paper from the pad and then walked over to Trisha to hand it to her; she took it and then thanked him. As Ryan walked back over to his desk, Trisha stood from the couch and then grabbed her purse again; Ryan turned around to her. "I was about to close the office, when you came, but if you'd like to continue talking, as friends, then we can go have dinner, if you want." Trisha nodded and slightly smiled. "Ok, that sounds good." Ryan slightly smiled too, and then grabbed his things; afterwards, both walked out his office together.

Chapter 3

Vance was sitting on the couch and leaned forward with his hands together; it was close to midnight and Trisha still wasn't home. He tried to call her several times and left text messages, but received no response. Since Trisha didn't have any friends, that he knew of, he had no one else to call.

Vance had been on that couch, for what seemed like forever. He heard the front door and then turned his head, as he stood from the couch. Trisha was about to walk by the living room, when she heard Vance. "Where've you been?" Trisha stopped and then turned her head; she slowly walked into the living room and over to him. Trisha shrugged her shoulders. "I needed some air, like I said." Vance frowned. "You needed air? For six damn hours? I've been calling and texting you for hours…I fed the kids, bathed them, and then put them to bed. After that, I was sitting here on the damn couch wondering where my damn wife was. So, where the hell did you go for this air?"

Trisha turned her head to the side and then back to Vance. "I drove around for hours, while thinking; I just needed time to myself." Vance stared at her and then slowly nodded his head. "You look like you've been crying…so," Trisha interjected. "I was driving, thinking, and crying…I'm exhausted now and I just wanna take a shower, before I go to bed." Vance shook his head and then slightly threw his hands up. "What's wrong, Trisha? You can talk to me, baby." Trisha shook her head. "No, I can't…goodnight, Vance." Trisha turned around and then walked out the living room, as he stood there and watched her. He rubbed his hands down his face and then decided to leave it alone for now; he didn't want to think the worst, but had a feeling that something wasn't right. Regardless, Vance was too tired to think any more about it; he had to get up for work in the morning and wanted to go to bed. Vance turned the lights out and then walked out the living room afterwards.

*   *   *

Cinco looked at the time and saw there was another couple of hours before the club closed; he was tired and ready to go home, but had to close. Joron was off tonight and both men still worked at the club; Cinco still tended the bar, with the other bartenders, unless needed elsewhere.

As he was cleaning a glass, someone squeezed through the crowd at the bar and then looked at Cinco. "Uh, excuse me…" Cinco looked up from the glass and looked at the guy. "What can I get you?" The guy nodded. "Are you the owner of the club?" Cinco shook his head. "No, but I'm the manager…so, do you need something?" The guy nodded his head. "So, the owner is not around?" Cinco set the glass down on the bar counter and then frowned, with the questions about the owner. "No, man; the owner is not around…he's usually not here at all, so if you need something, then you deal with me. Once again, what do you want?"

The guy slightly nodded his head. "Ok, well I was trying to see if maybe you had a job opening, that's all; I was hoping to see the owner, but I'll talk to you." Cinco sighed and then nodded. "We can always use the help…what can you do?" The guy slightly smiled. "I can do what you do…bartender." Cinco eyed the guy and then nodded. "Yeah alright, come back tomorrow and I'll give you an application to fill out." The guy nodded and then thanked Cinco; he was about to walk away, when Cinco stopped him. "Hey, what's your name?" The guy turned back around to Cinco. "It's Dean..." Cinco nodded and then Dean turned around to leave the bar; Cinco watched him and then got back to work.

A couple of hours later, the lights turned on and everyone knew it was time to go; it took twenty minutes to clear everyone out and afterwards, Cinco cleaned up and then made his rounds to make sure no one was left inside. About time Cinco was done, it was a little after three in the morning; he left the club, while dead tired and could barely keep his eyes open.

It didn't take him long to make it home; he parked in the driveway and then walked to the front door. Cinco yawned, as he unlocked the door and then went inside; he closed the door and then locked up, before walking to the bedroom. Cinco walked in the bedroom and saw Jordan asleep in the bed; he went to the bathroom and then took a quick shower, while trying to stay awake to finish. Afterwards, he exited the bathroom and then walked to the bed, to get in. Cinco got in the bed and then sighed.

Jordan felt moving in the bed and then rolled over; he moved closer to Cinco and then put his arm around him. Jordan woke up and then started to kiss Cinco on his neck; Cinco had his eyes closed and was about to be in a deep sleep, when Jordan moved his hand down in front of him. Cinco moved Jordan's hand from in front of him and spoke, with his eyes still closed. "I'm tired, Jordan…" Jordan ignored him and attempted to continue, when Cinco's tone became harsher. "Jordan, stop…I'm tired, man." Jordan frowned, as he slightly rose in the bed and looked at Cinco. "Are you serious?" Cinco opened his eyes and then turned his head, slightly, back to Jordan. "Yeah, I'm serious…it's almost four in the morning." Jordan frowned and then looked at the clock on the nightstand, before looking back at Cinco. "Why the hell did you get home so late?"

Cinco abruptly rose in the bed and then turned to Jordan. "Because I was working…what kind of question is that? I bust my ass at your club and stay after to clean up." Jordan continued to frown. "And what else do you do with your ass, at the club?" Cinco was outdone; he was too tired and sleepy to argue. "Nigga, are you for real?" Jordan sarcastically laughed.

"I'm a nigga now?" Cinco clenched his jaw, as he stared at Jordan. "Jordan, man…go to sleep." Jordan slowly nodded his head and then slightly laughed. "Sure, Cinco…I can do that." Jordan got out the bed, as Cinco watched him. "Where are you going, Jordan?" Jordan walked around the bed and made his way towards the door. "To get a damn drink and then go back to sleep in one of the other bedrooms." Cinco called his name, but Jordan ignored him, as he walked out the bedroom; he slammed the door behind him. Cinco sucked his teeth and then laid back down; he was on his back now and staring at the ceiling. He yawned again; although concerned about what just took place between him and Jordan, he had to get some sleep. Cinco rolled back over in the bed and then decided to address this the next day, with Jordan.

Chapter 4

It was the next day and Jaeda was in the kitchen, at Hawks. She was cooking with one of the other cooks, when a waitress walked in the back and called Jaeda's name. Jaeda looked up and then walked over to her. "Hey Jaeda, there's a guy out here, asking for you." Jaeda nodded and then the waitress left the kitchen; Jaeda spoke to one of the other cooks and then he nodded. Afterwards, Jaeda washed her hands and then walked out the kitchen; she looked around and then turned her head to see her guest.

Jaeda walked over to Daniel and then he turned around; he smiled and she did too. Daniel looked at her stomach and then shook his head. "I thought I saw a bump in that midsection at the wedding...so you're pregnant, huh?" Jaeda slightly laughed and then nodded, as she put her hand on her stomach. "Yeah, I'm seven months now." Daniel nodded and then asked if they could sit down and talk; she nodded and then looked around. Jaeda saw an empty table, by the window and then he followed her to the table.

Once at the table, Daniel pulled the chair out for her and then waited until she sat down, before sitting down in the other chair. Afterwards, he leaned forward on the table and then smiled. "Is this your place?" Jaeda sarcastically laughed and then shook her head. "Hell no, that ship sailed a long time ago…this is my friend's place and I work as a chef." He nodded and then grinned. "So, I got competition now, huh? I got a barbecue spot not too far from here…the other one's in Atlanta. Me and my brother moved to Houston to be closer to our dad, so we manage the spot here."

Jaeda sat back in the chair and then smiled, as she shook her head. "Wow, that's good; I knew you were the more talented one…" Daniel sucked his teeth, as he slightly leaned his head to the side. "Whatever, Jaeda…you were just as good as me, if not better; I just knew after you left, that you moved on to open your own spot. But I guess you changed your mind and decided to do the family thing…I hope not with Devonte."

Jaeda shook her head and then sighed. "Yeah, I had plans but they changed; and Devonte's been out of the picture for a while…prison now. I'm married to somebody else, and this is my third kid." Daniel nodded his head. "The only believable part is Devonte being in prison, but everything else about the kids is…I mean, I remember you saying you didn't want kids; I don't have any." Jaeda turned her head to the side and then back to Daniel. "Well, things changed…a lot. I don't have time to talk to you about everything right now; I gotta get back to work, so…" Daniel interjected. "No, that's cool…I understand; how about when you get some free time, you stop by my barbecue place and we can have a meal together, on me?" Jaeda smiled and then nodded. "Yeah, that sounds good; I'm off tomorrow, so is tomorrow good?" Daniel smiled and then nodded. "Yeah…" Jaeda said she had to get back to work, so she got up from the chair and he quickly got up from his chair to help her; afterwards, they hugged and then said, goodbye, before he walked away and left the restaurant.

While Jaeda stood there, Shavon went over to her and then looked in the direction that Jaeda was looking in. "Y'all looked cozy…" Jaeda turned her head to Shavon and then frowned. "That's Daniel, Miss Brooks' stepson…he's my friend from Atlanta, remember?" Shavon nodded, as she spoke. "Yeah, I remember…so, he just came to say a few words before going back to Atlanta?" Jaeda shook her head. "Uh no, he moved to Houston to be closer to his dad, but he has a spot in Atlanta now and one down here; a barbecue spot. He invited me for a meal, so since I'm off tomorrow, I'ma stop by." Shavon raised an eyebrow and then slowly nodded her head. "Uh, ok…well uh, you tell Joron about this dude?" Jaeda frowned and then shook her head, no. "I thought you were smarter than that, Shavon." Shavon laughed and Jaeda did too; Shavon put her hand up and then dropped it. "Enough said…I already know what the hell that means; anyway, be careful and take it easy…you still got a load in that belly." Jaeda rolled her eyes and then nodded. "I got it…I'm good and I'ma tell Joron, eventually, but there's nothing to tell anyway; me and Daniel were good friends and when I was going through everything, when I got back with Devonte, he was there for me." Shavon nodded and then looked around, before looking back at Jaeda. "Alright, girl…well, I'ma leave it alone; let's get back to work." Jaeda nodded and then both women returned to the kitchen.

Chapter 5

Cinco was getting ready for work in the bedroom, when Jordan arrived home; Jordan hung his keys on the wall and then walked to the living room. He set his briefcase by the couch and then started to undo his tie, as he walked to the bar. Cinco came out the bedroom, by this time and then made his way to the living room; he stopped and then slightly nodded. "I thought I heard you come in…" Jordan ignored Cinco and made his drink at the bar, as Cinco frowned. Cinco walked further in the living room and then over to Jordan; Jordan turned around at the bar and then sipped his drink, as he stared at Cinco.

Cinco slightly threw his hands up. "So, you're gonna ignore me or something?" Jordan shook his head. "There's nothing to ignore…have a good night at work." Jordan was about to walk around Cinco, when he was stopped. "Jordan, what's up with you? What was that shit after I got home this morning?" Jordan swallowed down the remainder of his drink and then sarcastically laughed. "You want to know what my problem is, huh? Ok, well, I'm sexually frustrated…the last time I went this long without sex, I was in the middle of a psychotic breakdown. Silly of me to think I would get more sex, after I was married, when that wasn't the case with Mya." Jordan laughed again and then walked around Cinco; he frowned and then turned around to Jordan. "Hold up, where the hell are you going with this, because I work and so do you? We're on two different schedules now since you got me managing your ex-boyfriend's club."

Jordan stopped in his tracks and then set the glass on the end table, before turning around to Cinco. Jordan wanted to tread lightly with his words, so he wouldn't say anything that he would regret, but he was angry now and wasn't sure he would be able to control himself. "Tyler was never my ex-boyfriend…and it's my club now, that I entrusted you to manage for me; something you were happy to do. And I am very much aware of our schedules…but it seems that since we became married, that you've been handling extra bullshit at the club that's not part of your job description. But I'm telling you this now, Cinco…the rules still apply, even now that we're married; pissing me off is your one-way ticket out of here."

Cinco raised an eyebrow, as he stared at Jordan and couldn't believe his last words to him; he slowly nodded his head and then walked over to Jordan. He slightly laughed and then shook his head. "I hate to remind you of this, Jordan…but I'm not Tyler or any of your other jilted exes and sidelines; I'm here with you because I wanna be, not because you want me to be…but I got no problem taking a walk, if you're kicking me out." Jordan stared at Cinco and then clenched his jaw; he then turned to walk away from Cinco, but Cinco grabbed his arm to stop him.

Jordan frowned, as he looked back at Cinco. "I suggest you let me go and take your ass to work." Cinco let Jordan go and then shook his head; he rubbed his hands down his face and then sighed. "Look Jordan, all I do is go to work and then come back home; there's no room for nothing in between. I know we're not having sex like we used to, but we both work different hours." He stepped closer to Jordan. "I'm just saying that I don't know what you thinking, but I'm not cheating, so don't go do something you're gonna regret." Jordan frowned and then stepped back from Cinco. "Do something I'm going to regret?" Cinco sighed and then turned his head to the side, as Jordan continued to frown. "Uh huh, so you're basically turning this around and advising me not to cheat on you." Jordan laughed and then Cinco turned his head back to him; Jordan shook his head, as he continued to laugh. "That is a good one, Cinco…once again, take your ass to work." Jordan turned around and then walked out the living room, while Cinco stood there and frowned; he then sucked his teeth, and grabbed his keys on the way out the house, to go to work.

Chapter 6

It didn't take Cinco long to get to work and after he parked, he got out his car and then went to the door, to unlock it. Cinco was about to go inside, when someone tapped him on the shoulder. Cinco turned around and saw Dean standing behind him. "Uh, Dean, right?" Dean nodded and then Cinco turned around to walk inside the club, with Dean behind him. Afterwards, Dean followed Cinco to his office, that Dean was familiar with, unbeknownst to Cinco.

Once in the office, Cinco went behind the desk. Dean slightly looked around and then went over to the chair to sit down. Cinco opened a drawer and then grabbed an application out to give to Dean. Dean thanked him and then grabbed a pen to start the application. Cinco grabbed his cellphone from his pocket and then started to look through it; he was trying to see if maybe Jordan sent him a text message, but he didn't. Cinco sighed and then looked up, after Dean started to speak. "This place looks good…I used to come here, but I hadn't been here in a few years."

Cinco looked at him and then nodded. "Oh, yeah?" Dean continued to fill out the application as he and Cinco talked. "Is that what the questions about the owner was about?" Dean looked at Cinco and then nodded. "Yeah…the last time I was here, that dude Tyler was the owner." Cinco nodded. "I don't know if you heard, but Tyler's dead and a friend of his, owns it now." Dean nodded his head. "Yeah, I did hear that; that's messed up…the place pretty much still looks the same, from when Tyler owned it." Cinco cleared his throat and then shrugged his shoulders. "I didn't know that…I wasn't around when Tyler owned this place."

Dean continued to fill out the application, as he spoke. "Yeah well, between me and you…I heard the new owner used to be Tyler's man and not just a friend. It makes sense if that's the deal, because everybody knew about them. I never saw two people so much in love, even when they tried to hide it. It's crazy because I remember people saying that after Tyler died, his man damn near lost his mind and never got over his death. It's good he kept Tyler's club and kept it going; some people just need something from the love of their life, to keep, when tragedies happen." Dean was almost done with the application, as Cinco stared at him; the conversation was irritating him and although he didn't want to hear anymore, he let Dean keep talking, in order to be nosey, since Jordan didn't speak about Tyler too much, unless asked. Cinco was still unaware of how deep their feelings were for each other, because Jordan refused to go in depth about it.

Cinco sighed and then nodded. "I didn't know nothing about that; I'm just the manager and I don't get in the owner's business like that." Jordan didn't want it to be known that he and Cinco were married; the only ones at the club that knew about them, were Joron and Vernon, whom didn't work at the club anymore.

Dean finished his application and then nodded, as he handed it back to Cinco. "Ok, well that makes sense to stay out the owner's business. If I was you, I wouldn't bring up Tyler to him anyway; I think he's still in love with him, from what people been saying. I heard he can't come here that much, because of the memories he had with Tyler; just too much for him." Cinco's entire demeanor changed and so did the expression on his face; he slowly nodded his head. Dean stared at him and then slightly leaned his head to the side. "Are you alright?"

Cinco nodded and attempted to go through the application, but couldn't concentrate now after hearing all that. He cleared his throat. "Yeah, I'm good; uh, so we do need people…more bartenders, so you're hired if you want the job." Dean smiled and then nodded. "Yeah, thanks, so when do I start?" Cinco stood from his chair, as Dean followed his lead. "You can start tonight…come back in another hour or if you're ready, you can just stick around until we open." Dean nodded and then slightly smiled. "That second part sounds better…I know we can't drink on the job, but if I say I'll start in another hour, then can we have a drink at the bar together now?" Cinco stared at him and then turned his head to the side; he then looked back at Dean. "Yeah, sure…come on." Cinco walked around Dean and then Dean followed him, with a grin on his face.

Chapter 7

Vance had left work and received a phone call from a colleague, while he was on his way home. Vance made a detour from his regular route home and went to another destination; when Vance reached the new destination, he parked and then looked around. Vance frowned and then squinted his eyes, to make sure he was seeing what he did. Vance saw Trisha and another man, sitting together outside, while talking on a restaurant patio.

Vance looked around and then back to Trisha and the unknown man; he took a deep breath and still didn't want to think the worst of his wife, but knew it was possible that she was having an affair. Vance wanted very much to jump out his car and bash his fist into the unknown man's face, especially while wondering where his children were, since it was obvious, they weren't with Trisha.

Vance took his cellphone from the console and then dialed his wife's number; he continued to stare at Trisha, as the phone rang. He witnessed Trisha take her cellphone from on top of the table and then answer. "Hello…" Vance nodded. "Hey, baby; I'm on my way home from work…let me hear my babies' voices." Trisha sat up straight in the chair, while Ryan watched her. "Oh, really? Right now?" Trisha stood from the chair and then grabbed her purse; Ryan stood from the chair too, as Vance nodded. "Yeah, I'm on my way now, so let me talk to my kids." Vance's tone was harsher, and Trisha could hear it. "They're taking a nap, but I'll make sure they're up when you get home." Vance slowly nodded his head. "Ok, well, I'll see you at home." Vance ended the call and then tossed his cellphone on the passenger seat; he was angry, so drove out the parking lot and then went home, while concerned about where his children were. Shortly after saying a few words to Ryan, Trisha quickly left to beat Vance home.

Sometime later, Vance had arrived home and was almost in a panic; he heard the children and made his way towards their laughing. Vance walked into the game room and then slowed down his pace; he saw the unknown woman with his twins and then frowned. "Who the hell are you?" The woman looked up at Vance, while playing on the floor with the twins. "I'm Maria…Mrs. Brooks' nanny." Vance raised an eyebrow. "Her nanny? Since when do we have a nanny? How long have you been working for my wife?" Maria realized who Vance was and then nodded. "I'm sorry,

Mr. Brooks…Mrs. Brooks just hired me; she called me this morning to watch the children. I'm very qualified, sir…" Vance sighed and then nodded. "Well, I appreciate you coming to watch my kids, but I'm home now, so you can leave. Did my wife pay you?" Maria stood from the floor and then nodded. "It's online payment, so she already paid me. I'm supposed to come back for the rest of the week, and until Mrs. Brooks tells me to stop." Vance clenched his jaw and then nodded. "Sure…you can leave now." Maria nodded; she waved to the children, before walking out the game room, and then leaving.

After she left, Vance walked over to his kids and then sat down on the couch; the twins got up from the floor and then went over to their daddy. Vance picked up the twins and had both of them on his lap; shortly after, Trisha was home and then walked from room to room, while calling out Maria's name. She didn't get a response, so became worried; she finally made it to the game room and then stopped when she saw Vance and the kids.

Vance turned his head to look at his wife; she slightly smiled. "Hey, I didn't think you would make it home before me." Vance put the twins down and then stood from the couch, as he continued to stare at her. "I bet you didn't. I walked in my house to see my kids with a stranger and not with their mama, so where were you and why did you lie to me?" Trisha sighed, as she walked in the game room and then stopped. "I had to step out for a minute and called Maria to come watch the kids." Vance slowly nodded his head and then swallowed hard. "Why didn't you tell me you hired a nanny? Why do you need one, when you're home all day?" Trisha slightly looked down and then back up again at Vance. "I decided to get a job, so I need a nanny to watch the kids while I go looking for one."

Vance frowned and stared at her, as if she lost her mind. "A job? So, now you wanna work...because from what I remember, you were allergic to work, when we were married the first time around?" Trisha swallowed hard and then nodded; she turned around and Vance cursed to himself. Vance quickly ran over to her, before Trisha walked out the game room; he turned her around. "Baby, I'm sorry...look, I'm just trying to understand what's going on with you. I wanna know where you went today, too." Trisha nodded. "I went out to look for a job today...and then stopped to get something to eat; I was eating something when you called. I lied because I didn't want you to know that I left the kids with a nanny."

Vance slowly nodded his head, as he stared at her. "So, you were by yourself all day?" Trisha slightly smiled and then nodded. "Yes, of course...I was by myself; I don't have any friends, remember, so who else would I be with?" Vance took a deep breath and then walked around Trisha, as he spoke. "Get the kids settled; I'm going to take a shower before dinner." Vance said nothing else, as she watched him walk out the game room. Afterwards, she looked back at the kids and then sighed.

Chapter 8

The club was packed and Joron was behind the bar with Dean, while attempting to train him; Cinco was in the office. Joron had no idea who this new guy was, but was getting irritated with him, while trying to work and train him, at the same time. Dean dropped a glass and Joron turned his head; he frowned and then went over to him. "Dude, come on now; that's the third damn glass you broke." Dean sighed and then shook his head. "I'm sorry, I'm gonna get the hang of this." Joron frowned. "Get the hang of it? How the hell you get this job, with no damn experience?"

By this time, Cinco walked to the bar and then saw Joron in Dean's face; he went behind the bar and then went over to the men. "Hey, what's going on?" Both men looked at him and then Joron sucked his teeth.

"I'll tell you what's going on, this nigga don't know what the fuck he's doing. Why did you hire him?" Cinco frowned, as he stared at Joron. "Ron, are you for real? You didn't have no damn experience either, when you started working here, but your ass still behind the bar." Joron gave Cinco a snide look. "I got more experience than this nigga and I didn't have to break three damn glasses to prove anybody wrong." Joron walked away from both of them and then Cinco sighed, as he looked at Dean. "Don't worry about Ron; he's a little high strung sometimes."

Dean laughed and Cinco did too; he went to grab the broom and dustpan, to sweep up the glass, as Dean stood by. "I'm real sorry…maybe I should of said I don't have much experience." Cinco shrugged his shoulders. "No problem…I can train you, if Ron don't want to." Dean stepped closer to Cinco. "I'm hoping you do." Cinco looked at Dean and then cleared his throat; he nodded. "Yeah, alright…" Cinco finished sweeping up the glass and then disposed of it. Afterwards, he got back to Dean; both walked over to the bar counter and then Cinco started to train Dean.

As the guys were together, Joron finished with a patron and then turned his head; he did a doubletake and then frowned, when he saw the close proximity that Cinco and Dean were to each other. He went to help another patron and about time he finished, he turned his head back to the guys again and was outdone with what he was seeing. He saw Cinco put his hand over Dean's while working the beer tap.

Joron had enough and then walked over to the guys. "You niggas having fun?" Both guys turned to Joron and Cinco moved back from Dean. "Ron, what's your problem, man?" Joron looked at Dean and then back to Cinco. "You want me to say it in front of everybody or take this shit to your office?" Cinco looked at Dean and then excused him and Joron; the guys walked away, as Dean watched them.

After they walked in the office, Cinco couldn't get a word in, before Joron started up. "What the fuck you doing out there with that dude?" Cinco frowned, as he stared at Joron. "I'm not doing nothing; what's wrong with you?" Joron made a sarcastic sound. "Well from where I was standing it looked like you was doing a lot. Training somebody don't involve touching…so, why did you really hire that no experienced nigga?" Cinco shook his head and then sarcastically laughed. "I think you paying a little bit too much attention to what I'm doing and not enough on your job. You're the one that acted an ass out there, because he dropped a few glasses; it's his first night, Ron. All I'm doing is what you should of been out there doing…training him."

Joron stepped closer to Cinco and then slightly leaned his head to the side, as he stared at him. "My job ain't to train that nigga, but it is to watch out for my brother, so I'm just letting you know that now, in case you're confused about the shit. Me and you cool, but that shit can change real quick, if I find out you fuckin' with that nigga out there." Joron said nothing else, as he turned around and then walked out the office; he slammed the door.

Cinco sighed and then rubbed his hands down his face. It was bad enough that he and Jordan were in conflict, but he didn't expect him and Joron to be in conflict as well. Cinco decided to just stay away from Dean from now on, before something else was seen by Joron or another patron, that was misunderstood. The last thing Cinco needed, was for Jordan to be informed of a misunderstanding between him and Dean. After Cinco got himself together, he left the office to get back to work.

As the night progressed, Cinco attempted to stay away from Dean for the remainder of the night, while under Joron's watchful eye. Dean noticed what was going on and also stayed away from Cinco, so as to not cause any trouble. As soon as Joron stepped away from the bar, Dean walked over to Cinco and then looked around again, before looking back at him. "Hey, I noticed that Ron came out the office earlier, pissed off, than before he went in. Is everything alright?" Cinco looked at Dean and then nodded. "Yeah, we're good…a little misunderstanding, but it's good now. Look, when Ron's around, we just need to keep our distance." Dean slowly nodded his head. "Is there a reason for that? I mean, y'all not together or something, are y'all?" Cinco frowned and then shook his head. "No, that's not it…he's just the brother of the owner; the owner don't like co-workers to be, uh socializing with each other, so me and you can't be that close."

Dean slightly laughed and then nodded. "Brother, huh? Ok, well, I didn't know we were getting close…" Cinco stared at Dean and then cleared his throat. "We're not, just a warning…so something like that won't happen." Dean eyed Cinco and then nodded. "I understand and I'll be sure to keep my distance…if I can." Dean turned around and then walked away from Cinco. Cinco sighed and then got back to work.

A few hours went by and it was closing time again. Joron left, after the partygoers, along with other staff. Cinco was in his office and about to make rounds, after being notified that everyone was gone; he was about to walk out the office, when there was a knock at the door. Cinco opened the door and saw Dean. "Uh, hey, man." Dean nodded. "I just wanted to let you know that I can help you clean up, so you don't have to be here too long; one of the guys told me that you don't usually leave until about after three." Cinco nodded. "Yeah, thanks…I can really use the help."

Dean nodded and then cleared his throat. "Uh, I'm not trying to lose my job or anything, but I just wanted to let you know that I'm into guys…and I'm thinking you are too; I just got a vibe and felt something when you were training me." Cinco shook his head. "No, well yeah, I'm into guys, but I wasn't trying nothing with you…" Dean slowly nodded his head. "Let me guess…a misunderstanding, right? It's cool, Cinco, I get it…but in case you change your mind I just want you to know that I'm interested." Cinco sighed and before he could respond, Dean stepped closer to Cinco and then kissed him; as much as Cinco wanted to push Dean away, he couldn't. Cinco hadn't had this much affection in a while, so let the kiss linger.

When Dean tried to go further, Cinco then got his mind right; he slightly pushed Dean back and then slightly put fingers to his mouth. "Dean, come on…we can't do that again." Dean nodded and then cleared his throat. "I'm sorry, I won't do it again…just let me help you clean up and then we can go." Cinco sighed and then nodded; both men, then left the office, to make rounds and clean up.

Chapter 9

It was the weekend and Vance's thirty-fourth birthday party; Jorvik had turned thirty-four in the middle of the week and once again, the guys decided to have a joint party. The party was at Jorvik and Arianna's home; everyone's children were brought to the house, except for Jaeda and Joron's kids. Rydell and Giani were keeping the kids, while they attended the party. Arianna had a nanny upstairs to watch the other children in the game room, that was converted into a playroom. Vance and Trisha arrived, while both had other things on their minds. Jordan and Cinco were there, Randy and Shavon, Lillian and Lawrence, and even Dimitri and Valerie were in town, and at the party.

Everyone seemed to be having a good time; Valerie, Shavon, and Jaeda were together while Dimitri, Jordan, Arianna, Vance, Joron, and Jorvik were together. Cinco had walked away to new guests that arrived, which were Lawrence's sons, Eljay and Daniel; Jaeda was unaware that he was going to be at the party, but decided to speak to him a little later. Randy, Lawrence and Lillian were also with them.

Everyone seemed to be in their own circles and grouped, except for Trisha. As the guys and Arianna were standing together, Dimitri smiled, as he looked around at everyone, but his smile slightly faded, as he saw some didn't have happy looks on their faces. Dimitri cleared his throat. "Ok, so what's the matter with some of you?" Vance looked at Dimitri, as he sipped his drink. "I think Trisha is cheating on me…" The guys shot him a look and Jordan sighed. "I think Cinco is cheating on me." The guys looked back at Jordan. Arianna frowned. "And so it begins…" Vance shot Arianna a look. "What is that supposed to mean?" Arianna looked between Jordan and Vance. "I'm just saying…you two have experience with infidelity, so if you feel your spouses are cheating, then I'm sure they are." Jorvik frowned, as he looked at Arianna. Jordan rolled his eyes, while Joron slightly laughed.

Vance shook his head. "Thank you, Arianna, I don't know what I would do if I didn't have a friend like you." Dimitri laughed and so did Joron. Arianna gave Vance a snide look; she then shook her head. "Come on, Vance…you remarried a woman that you told to her face, you were cheating on; and Shavon is standing on the other side of the room, with the previous ex-sidelines, while you're here with Trisha. It can't get any worse than that…and you guys already know that someone would die, if Vik had his ex-wife here, in my damn house, and was talking about being friends."

The guys frowned, as Jorvik put his hand up and then dropped it. "Uh baby, please leave me out of your rant on fidelity; we don't have these types of problems." Vance rolled his eyes, as Jordan told his brother to shut up. Jorvik sighed, as Arianna shook her head, and continued to sip her drink.

Dimitri looked at Vance and then sighed. "Don't listen to Arianna. The last time we spoke, you said everything was good; how do you know she's cheating on you?" Vance sipped his drink and then looked around at everyone. "I saw her with another man…they were talking and then I called her phone; she lied about what she was doing and even hired a nanny behind my back, so she can be out during the day, without me knowing. She's been acting weird for a while, since my mama's wedding. I know this can happen, but I don't want to believe it." The guys shook their heads and didn't know what to say to that.

Jordan cleared his throat. "Me and Cinco haven't had sex in about a month and a half." Dimitri choked on his drink, as Joron and Jorvik frowned. Arianna slightly laughed, as Vance sighed. Jorvik shook his head. "I think you're paranoid, Jordan…Cinco loves you and just because you two aren't having sex, doesn't mean, he's cheating." Joron made a sarcastic sound and everyone looked at him. Joron looked around at everyone and then shook his head. "Uh nah man, I don't think Cinco cheating neither." Before another word could be said, Cinco spoke. "What?" Everyone turned to him and Jordan sighed.

Cinco looked around at everyone and then to Jordan. "So, you're going around telling everybody that I'm cheating on you?" Jordan gave Cinco a snide look. "I never said you were cheating…I said I think you are cheating." Jorvik put his hand over his face, as Cinco slowly nodded his head. "Yeah ok, or maybe you're just feeling some type of way, because you miss the love of your fucking life, Tyler." Jordan frowned, as everyone looked at Cinco. He had what Dean disclosed to him, on his mind.

Jordan sarcastically laughed, but before he could speak, Cinco did again. "Is something funny, Jordan? Maybe what's funny is the fact that you can't even walk in your own damn club, without thinking about your lost love." Jordan looked around at everyone and then back to Cinco. "What the hell are you talking about? And why the hell are you talking about Tyler so much? I don't talk about Tyler and haven't in a long time, so what is wrong with you?" Cinco became enraged. "That's the fucking point!" Jordan was outdone, as Jorvik cleared his throat, and the others slightly looked at Jordan.

Cinco looked around at everyone and then back to Jordan. "I'm going to the club…" Before Cinco could walk away, Jordan spoke. "For what? Who the hell is there that is so important where you need to be there tonight?" Cinco looked at Joron, and Joron slightly frowned; Cinco looked back at Jordan. "Nobody…but you're gonna make me say something that I know I'ma regret, if I stay here." Jordan stepped closer to Cinco.

"Like what? You should know by now that words like that, don't mean anything to me." Jorvik and the others thought that Jordan and Cinco should stop before words were actually said, that couldn't be taken back.

Cinco swallowed hard and then shook his head. "I'm starting to think I'm just another Nick to you…just like all the other notches on your fucking headboard. Stupid of me to think I was gonna be different. I'm not cheating on you and I'm tired of saying that shit to you and Ron, but I swear, Jordan, if you go back to your old ways of fucking everything moving, because of false beliefs, then I'm gone." Cinco turned around and then stormed out of the living room, as Jordan watched him and others. Jordan swallowed down the remainder of his drink and then shot his brother a look.

Jordan continued to stare at Joron, as everyone else in the group did; Joron sucked his teeth, as Jordan shook his head. "What the fuck is he talking about? When did he have to tell you, he wasn't cheating?" Joron sighed and then shrugged his shoulders. "It's a new dude that works at the club; he's a bartender, but his work is shit. I don't know why Cinco hired him, but I don't like him. I thought they were a little close to each other, when Cinco was training him, so I said something to him. He said it wasn't my business and they wasn't doing nothing, so I hadn't brought it up to Cinco since; but after our little chat, they all of a sudden been staying away from each other when I'm around. I know it's because Cinco don't want me to tell."

Jordan frowned and then looked at Jorvik, before looking back at Joron. "Are you serious? Why didn't you tell me?" Joron threw his hand up. "There's a chance they're not doing nothing, that's why. I already told that nigga I better not catch his ass doing something he ain't got no business doing with that dude. I just saw them a little too close, that's it." Jordan shook his head and then said he was going to get another drink; Joron called his name, but Jordan ignored him. Dimitri sighed, as Arianna lit a cigarette.

Chapter 10

Trisha walked over and Vance turned his head to her. "What's wrong?" Trisha glanced around at everyone and then looked back at Vance. "I'm leaving…" Vance rolled his eyes and then shook his head. "What is the damn problem now?" Dimitri frowned, while Arianna raised an eyebrow of how Vance was speaking to Trisha; she slightly frowned and then cleared her throat. "I'm tired and I wanna go home, so I'm leaving; I called an Uber and me and the kids are leaving. You stay and have a good night." She was about to walk away, when Vance grabbed her arm. Dimitri shook his head, as Trisha frowned. Vance had enough of this. "Why is it such a big deal for you to be with me anywhere, when I'm around my friends and family?"

Trisha snatched her arm from Vance and then slightly laughed. "Friends and family, huh? When are you going to open your eyes, Vance? Your friends are the husbands of my former friends, their former wives. I'm a joke to them and to their new wives…that just treated me like shit; and I'm paraphrasing here, of what Shavon told me, but basically, I will never be accepted as your wife as far as she or anyone else is concerned. I come with you to parties and events, where I'm ostracized and treated once again, like I'm beneath you. And you just blow it off like it's my fault, when I've been desperately trying to fit in with people who don't want me around. This was a mistake and we should have never gotten remarried. I'm fine raising my children on my own."

Trisha didn't realize that she was crying, so she quickly wiped her eyes and attempted to retreat, when Vance stopped her. "Who is the guy that you lied to me about being with, the other day? Are you having an affair with him?" Trisha looked at Vance and then frowned, since it was obvious that he didn't hear or listen to a word that she just said. She sighed and then shook her head, no. "He is my therapist and we haven't had sex with each other in over two years." Trisha said nothing else, as she walked away from Vance and then went to get the kids.

Vance stood there and processed everything she said, but was more so disturbed with her last words. Jordan had returned to hear the majority of what was said between the spouses. Dimitri rubbed his hand down his face, as Vance looked around at all of them. "Did she just say that she hasn't had sex with her therapist in over two years? She's cheating on me with her therapist?" Jorvik sighed, as Vance looked over at Shavon and the others; he saw the women staring at him, and became enraged.

Trisha walked from downstairs and had the kids with her; Vance tried to speak to her, but she refused to hear anything he had to say. Vance then looked back at the women and handed his glass to Jorvik. Dimitri frowned, as the others wondered what he was about to do. Vance spoke, as he stared at the women. "Dimitri…Ron…I suggest you two go collect your wives, before they get their feelings hurt, along with Shavon." Arianna raised an eyebrow and then looked at Dimitri and Joron; Jordan and Jorvik followed her lead. Dimitri frowned. "Vance, come on…" Vance shot Dimitri a look. "Come on what, Dimitri? I didn't get remarried to Trisha for this to happen, for her to feel like this whenever we all get together." Arianna sighed. "Really, Vance? She knew what she was getting back into when she became your wife again."

Vance shot her a look. "Oh yeah, Arianna? And what is that? What the hell was she getting into by marrying me again? The chance to be happy this time around? You're full of shit, Arianna, and always have been. You're the reason Ethan lost his mind the way he did, because you're a bitch. I see you haven't learned a damn thing from all of this. You strung him along for so damn long, and made him think he had a chance with you, but you always knew that was never going to happen." Arianna interjected. "Wait a minute, Vance…" Vance shot back. "Shut up!" Arianna closed her mouth, and Vance sarcastically laughed, as he looked at Joron and Dimitri. "You two must think I'm playing right now too…"

Vance turned around and then made his way over to Shavon and the others. Dimitri opened his mouth to speak and then closed it. Joron rubbed his hands down his face. "Fuck..." Jordan shook his head, as Jorvik looked at Arianna; she looked at him and then sighed.

Chapter 11

Vance made his way over to Shavon and then everyone looked at him; by this time, Daniel, Eljay, Randy, Lillian, and Lawrence were with Valerie, Jaeda, and Shavon.

Shavon looked at Vance, as he stared angrily at her. "What did you tell my wife?" Shavon looked at the women and then slightly laughed, as she looked back at Vance. "You mean, what I told Trisha?" Vance leaned his head to the side, as Randy looked at her. Vance clenched his jaw. "Trisha, huh? That would be my wife, Shavon…unless you conveniently forgot what it means when you get married to someone." Shavon raised an eyebrow, as the women kept quiet. Randy intervened. "Vance, come on, we all saw your wife leave with the kids, but you can't take that out on Shavon." Vance shot Randy a look. "I suggest you stay out of this, Randy, because you don't know what the hell is going on."

Vance looked back at Shavon. "Since you don't wanna talk, Shavon, then I'll do it for you; Trisha said you and the other ex-sidelines treated her like shit…like she's not welcome to even be a friend to any of you." Randy frowned, as he looked at Shavon. Jaeda sighed, while Lillian raised an eyebrow and also looked at Shavon.

Shavon cleared her throat. "That's not what I said." Vance grit his teeth. "Then what did you say?!" Everyone jumped when Vance yelled. Shavon looked at Randy and then back to Vance; she shrugged her shoulders. "I just told her that she can't hang with us…I mean, just because you married her again, don't mean she's accepted by us now. It's weird anyway…" Lillian shook her head, as Jaeda knew that Shavon was wrong.

Vance frowned, and this was the part that he warned Dimitri and Joron about. "Is that right? She's not accepted because she's my wife again? She's not accepted because of what, Shavon? You're the only one without a damn ring on your finger…out of everyone, so if anything, you should be the one not accepted. Whose fucking wife, are you?" Shavon opened her mouth and Randy tried to speak, but Lillian told him to shut up too; he sighed and Shavon slightly nodded her head. "So, now you gonna be cold and cruel to me, because your wife's feelings were hurt?" Vance was outdone by this conversation. "You don't get it, Shavon…I changed, but I see you didn't. I love my wife and my children; I chose to put a ring on her finger again, because I love her that much. She expressed to me how she's been treated by the ex-sidelines, when she is the one that has to look at your face…the woman that I cheated on her with. She is the one that tried to be your friend and you treated her like shit, when you are the reason for the end of my marriage to her in the first place!" Lawrence glanced at Lillian, as she kept quiet and glanced at Randy; he said nothing. Shavon looked around at everyone and her feelings were hurt now, but Vance wasn't finished.

Vance looked between Jaeda and Valerie. "And you two…." Jaeda put her hand up and then shook her head. "No, don't Vance…the bad treatment towards Trisha, wasn't from me." Shavon looked at Jaeda and frowned, as Valerie did as well. "Really, Jaeda?" Jaeda frowned, as she looked at Valerie. "Yeah Val, really." Vance looked at Valerie. "You know what, it's good that none of you don't want Trisha around, because I don't want her around any of you bitches anyway." Vance turned around and said nothing else, as he walked away from the group.

After he was gone, Valerie and Shavon shot Jaeda a look; Shavon spoke. "So, you just threw us under the bus?" Jaeda frowned, as she looked at Shavon. "Are you for real, Shavon? I told you not to do Trisha like that. I was Trisha at one time…I know how it feels to be with somebody, who's cheating on me…you don't. All I did was be with a man that used to be my damn husband in the first place. If I hadn't of gotten my memory back, then we'd of stayed married. Val fucked her sister's husband and you decided that Vance's wife wasn't the right woman for him, so decided to be his bitch on the side. Vance was right, you don't have a right to treat Trisha like shit, when you're the only one that's not even a wife. You don't even care how she feels having to see your face all the time…and then you do her like that. You act like you're mad about Vance getting back with Trisha and marrying her again; maybe you're jealous that he still wanted her after all the work you put in, for him to be yours. Now they're married again with kids, so big surprise you're acting a damn ass towards her." Jaeda walked away from all of them without saying another word.

After Jaeda left, Valerie was now embarrassed. Shavon turned her head and saw Randy staring at her; he heard everything that was said and was getting a clearer picture of what was going on. Shavon sighed. "Maybe we should leave." Randy made a sarcastic sound. "You think, Shavon?" Shavon sighed, as Randy looked at his mama and then walked away; Shavon went after him. Vance had already left the party and made his way home; he couldn't stomach staying in the same room with Shavon anymore.

Daniel had hoped that he would get the chance to speak to Jaeda tonight, but would obviously wait until another time, because of what happened and because she was with her husband. Lillian knew it would be a matter of time before this situation came to light and would attempt to speak to the women another time. Not too long after, the party died down; everyone went to get their children and then leave, after their goodbyes. Arianna and Jorvik went upstairs to relieve the nanny and then put Evan to bed, before they took a shower and then did the same.

Chapter 12

Vance went home and then called out for Trisha; he saw her SUV outside, so knew that she was home. Vance continued to call out for her and then went to the kids' bedroom. He stopped when he walked inside and then frowned. "Trisha, what are you doing?" Trisha turned her head from the bed. She was packing the twins' bags, and had already packed hers; Trisha's things were already in the SUV.

Trisha stopped what she was doing. "I'm leaving…I need time to myself to think about what I wanna do." Vance frowned, as he walked into the bedroom, and then shook his head. "Leaving? Where are you going? If this is about what happened, I'm telling you that I took care of it." Trisha sighed, as she looked down and then back up again at Vance. "You didn't take care of anything, Vance. I am tired of being a joke to everyone…I am tired of my feelings being ignored, and I am tired of this marriage."

Vance shook his head, no. "Baby, I'm sorry, but I don't want you to leave. I mean, where are you going to go?" Trisha shrugged her shoulders. "I have a friend that offered me a place to stay with the kids, if I ever needed it." Vance frowned. "What friend? The therapist that you're cheating on me with? You're not about to take my kids and go stay with some dude that you're fucking." Trisha stared at him and then shook her head. "Do you really want to fight in front of the kids? Or maybe it's possible that you could think about me for once and not just yourself…and let me go." Vance stared at her and frowned. "I haven't been thinking about myself since we were married; I've been thinking about you and the kids. You didn't even deny you're cheating on me!"

The twins were standing in the bedroom and looked at their daddy, after his outburst; Trisha looked at them and then back to Vance. "I'm not cheating, so leave me alone and let me leave with my kids." Tears fell from Trisha's eyes and Vance slightly nodded his head. "Fine…if you need time, then take it." Vance turned around and then walked out the bedroom in a hurry, because he was about to lose it; he went to his bedroom and then slammed the door.

Trisha got back to packing the twins' bags and after she was finished, she left the house with the twins. Vance was in his bedroom and sitting on the side of the bed; he was distraught that his wife and kids were gone and couldn't help thinking that this was how Trisha must have felt, when he left her. It was a horrible feeling to have the one you loved leave you. The fact that Vance had no idea where she was going and who she was going to be with, was another reason, he was saddened. Vance rubbed his hands down his face and then laid back on the bed; he stared at the ceiling while in a trance and felt this was a horrible birthday.

Chapter 13

Ryan opened the door and then slightly frowned; he quickly took one of the sleeping twins from Trisha, as she held the other. Ryan moved out the way, so Trisha could walk in. "Trisha, it's late…what are you doing out with the kids?" After she walked in, he closed the door and then looked at her, with Vander asleep on his shoulder. "I'm sorry, but I didn't have anywhere else to go; I was hoping your offer for a place to stay was…" Ryan interjected. "Yeah, of course…come on." Ryan walked away from the front, with Trisha behind; she followed him to a downstairs bedroom, where he opened the door and then walked in, with her behind. Ryan went over to the bed and then laid Vander down; Trisha laid Tristan down and then tucked them both in, under the covers. Afterwards, both quietly walked out the bedroom and then Ryan cracked the door.

Both walked to his living room and then over to the couch; they sat down and then Ryan looked at her. "Do you wanna talk about it…or maybe wait until tomorrow?" Trisha sat back against the couch and then shook her head. "Tonight, was Vance's birthday party…at one of his friend's houses, Arianna." Ryan nodded and then sighed; Trisha had talked about all of Vance's friends in past sessions. Trisha continued. "Everyone had their own cliques and friends…and once again, I was alone; the kids even had other kids to play with. But not me…I stood alone and by myself the entire time. I tried to go over to the new wives, or ex-sidelines, to be friends with them, but they rejected me. Shavon did all the talking for her and the others, and basically said I would never be accepted." Ryan sighed and then shook his head. "Trisha…" She interjected. "I know what you are going to say, but I did try…for Vance and me. I just wanted the past to be the past, and was willing to overlook that Shavon was my husband's ex-sideline, just to be liked."

Ryan shook his head and was disgusted. "You can't keep putting aside your damn feelings for others; you spent your entire life doing that…if not with your parents, then for Vance, and now for a woman that doesn't give a damn about you and never did. You have children now, Trisha…you have to be strong for them and show them, that their mama is not weak. Love is not enough to change someone and it's surely not the only reason to stay in a marriage." Trisha looked at Ryan and then slightly smiled; she then slightly laughed. "I swear to you, Ryan, that this wasn't the plan. I thought it would be different this time around with Vance. I thought he really loved me; now I'm not sure what to think. Maybe if I hadn't have gotten pregnant, then we wouldn't be married again now. I just don't know, but you're right, because I don't want my kids to grow up this way."

Ryan nodded and then turned his head to the side, before looking back at her. "Uh, I know we haven't talked about it and I understand that it might not be appropriate, right now, but I have to say something." Trisha stared at him and he sighed. "Well, the day you walked out my office…more so ran out my office, I did end things with my wife. I went home that evening and told her that I had an affair with another woman. I didn't tell her that you were a patient, just someone that I fell in love with; we divorced within the next two months. But I never got the chance to apologize to you, for lying about my marital status. I never meant to lie to you or hurt you, but I couldn't help how you made me feel. I couldn't understand how a man could treat you the way Vance did." Trisha turned away from Ryan and then sighed; it wasn't planned and Trisha was vulnerable at the time, while longing for someone's love and acceptance as she did her entire life.

Trisha nodded her head, as she looked back at him. "I understand and it's fine, Ryan; things happen…I just wish we had met under different circumstances and I wasn't always crying, like I am now, every time we saw each other." She slightly laughed and he did too. Ryan looked down and then back up again at her. "I never stopped thinking about you and I still love you; I'm also here for you and you can stay as long as you need, with the kids." Trisha smiled, as she stared at him. "Thank you…" She leaned in to hug him and the gesture was embraced; they slightly pulled back from each other and Ryan looked into her eyes. He leaned back in, but not for another hug, but instead to kiss her; it started slow and then it became deeper. Ryan moved Trisha back on the couch and was about to lay her all the way back on the couch, when she stopped him. "Wait Ryan, 1 can't..." Ryan moved back up from her and then cleared his throat. "I'm sorry..." Trisha rose back up on the couch and then shook her head. "Don't be...it was nice." Ryan slightly smiled and then nodded; he then stood from the couch. "How about we go to bed? You can stay in the bedroom with the twins and tomorrow, we can talk some more." She nodded and then stood from the couch; Ryan walked her to the bedroom and then afterwards, he went upstairs to go to bed.

Chapter 14

Cinco was at the club and had what was going on between him and Jordan, on his mind. It was another packed night and Cinco was just happy that Joron wasn't there since he took off to go to Vance and Jorvik's party. Cinco continued to help patrons, while tending the bar; he then turned his head and saw Dean make his way over to him. Dean stopped when he reached Cinco and then smiled. "Hey, you look like shit…" Cinco rolled his eyes and then slightly laughed. "Thanks…" Cinco walked around Dean and then went to help another patron; Dean turned around to face him and then sighed, as a patron asked for a drink, from Dean.

After a few more minutes of helping patrons, the guys finally stopped and were able to talk. Dean stood next to Cinco and then shrugged his shoulders. "I'm sorry, I saw you looking like your dog died, so I just wanted to make you laugh." Cinco sighed and then shook his head. "No problem; I'm alright…I just got some shit on my mind." Dean nodded and then sighed. "Ok, well since I been staying with you after closing, we been knocking out cleaning up pretty quick; maybe after we close tonight and finish up, you might wanna come by my place and have a drink." Cinco looked at him and then back straight; he then cleared his throat and then shook his head, no. "I can't do that…" Cinco walked around Dean and then from behind the bar; he was going to go to the office. Dean also walked from behind the bar and then went down the hall towards the back.

Cinco walked in the office and was about to close the door, when Dean stopped it with his hand. Cinco turned to see Dean walk in and then close the door behind him. "Cinco…I'm sorry." Cinco looked at Dean and then shook his head. "Dean, man…I said I can't do this. I got too much shit on my damn mind to think about doing what I know you want." Dean nodded and then stepped closer to Cinco. "Yeah, and I think I know what's on your mind…what's his name?" Cinco frowned, as he stared at Dean; he then shook his head. "How do you know it's some dude that's on my mind?" Dean laughed and then raised an eyebrow, as he looked at Cinco. "Come on, Cinco…what happened? You can tell me."

Cinco rubbed his hands down his face and then went over to the couch, to sit down; Dean followed his lead and sat down next to him. Cinco sighed and then looked at Dean. "I don't really wanna talk about him like that, but we're just not on the same page right now; we're not having sex because of our schedules and he's more frustrated and pissed about it, then me. He's just not used to that; I think he got more exes and lovers than me and you combined."

Dean slightly frowned and then slightly laughed, as Cinco did too; he sat back against the couch and then sighed, as Dean looked at him. "There's no damn way time can't be made for sex…between two people. My ex always made time for sex…we both had a great sex life with each other; it was just…we did everything too." Dean drifted off into thought, as Cinco looked at him and then raised an eyebrow. "You alright?" Dean snapped out of his thoughts and then looked at Cinco. "Uh yeah, I was just thinking…" Cinco laughed and then shook his head. "I can see that…it looks like you were thinking about sex with your ex, a little too hard." Dean laughed and Cinco joined him; Dean stopped and then nodded. "I just miss him…I still love him and I wish we were still together; it was my fault that it ended, at least that's what I keep telling myself to make sense of what happened between us."

Cinco nodded and then Dean smiled at him. "I hadn't been with anybody since him and it's been a while…I understand what you're going through between you and your man." Cinco nodded and then Dean sighed; both guys stared at each other and then Dean leaned in to kiss Cinco. Before their talk, Cinco would have pushed Dean back from him, but after their talk, it was apparent to Cinco, that he and Dean needed this, again. The guys kissed harder and then Dean moved even closer to Cinco; Cinco laid back on the couch and Dean was all the way over him. Dean rose up to pull his shirt over his head and then went back down to Cinco. It became more intense than Cinco had expected, but it had also been so long since Cinco had sex. Dean and Cinco moved fast to remove and undo clothing; it wasn't too long after that both engaged in sexual activity while on the couch, in the office.

Chapter 15

It was the next day and Jordan had already gotten up to take his shower; he was in the bathroom, when Cinco walked in the bedroom and went to the dresser to take his watch and ring off. Jordan walked out the bathroom with a towel around his waist and then saw Cinco at the dresser; he walked over to the dresser as well to get some underwear. Cinco glanced at Jordan, who ignored him. Cinco stood there and then Jordan dropped his towel; he then put his underwear on and turned to Cinco when he finished. "Another late night?" Cinco looked at Jordan and then nodded. "Uh yeah, the club was packed." Jordan stared at Cinco for a few seconds and then walked around him.

Cinco turned around to him. "So, we're still doing this?" Jordan stopped and then sarcastically laughed, with his back turned to Cinco. "You threw a damn tantrum last night and made an ass out of me, in front of my friends. So, what exactly are we still doing?" Jordan turned around to Cinco. Cinco stared at Jordan and then cleared his throat. "Uh, yeah about last night; I'm sorry…so maybe we can forget it ever happened." Jordan stared at Cinco and then slightly leaned his head to the side. "Uh huh…" Jordan walked over to the bed and then put his basketball shorts on. Cinco turned to him and then sighed. Cinco decided to leave it alone and then the doorbell rang; he walked out the bedroom, as Jordan finished getting himself together.

Cinco went to the door and then opened it to find Dimitri and Vance; he nodded to them and then stepped aside, so they could walk in. Cinco was about to close the door, when Joron, Jorvik and Arianna walked in; they had Evan with them. Afterwards, Cinco closed the door and then walked back towards the bedroom; Jordan walked out and then glanced at Cinco, before he continued to walk past him and to the living room. Cinco sighed and then went to the bedroom, to watch television in there.

Jordan walked in the living room and then frowned, when he saw the looks on everyone's faces. He cleared his throat and everyone looked at him. Jordan shook his head, as he went over to the bar. "I see everyone had a rough night…at least I'm not the only one." Dimitri made a sarcastic sound. "You got that right?" Vance glanced at Arianna, and she glanced at him. Jordan turned around at the bar and frowned at Dimitri. "What's wrong with you?" Dimitri sighed.

"Apparently after me and Val left the party last night…she had words for me, thanks to Vance." Vance looked at him and then rolled his eyes. Dimitri shook his head. "Even though Vance made Shavon feel like shit, apparently Jaeda continued where Vance left off and had words for the women too." Joron frowned, as Jordan shook his head.

Vance threw his hands up. "Whatever, I don't care how Shavon or anyone else feels…Trisha left me and took the kids." Everyone looked at him and Jordan sighed, as he went to sit down on the couch. Arianna looked at Jorvik and then back to Vance. "I'm sorry, Vance." Vance shot her a look. "Really, Arianna?" She threw her hands up, as Evan slept against Jorvik's chest. "Ok, on behalf of all of us, I'm sorry, Vance…really. We're friends and when I was with Ethan and Marc, all of you tolerated them, so it's only fair that we do the same for you." Jorvik and the others frowned, with Arianna's speech.

Arianna looked around at all of them and then frowned too. "What?" Vance rolled his eyes, as Jordan slightly laughed. "Just take it, Vance…that's the best apology you are going to get from Arianna." Dimitri and Jorvik laughed, as Arianna crossed her arms. Vance rubbed his hands down his face and then sighed. "She left with my kids…I don't know where she went or who she's with, but I can take a guess, since she already admitted she cheated on me with her therapist." Dimitri frowned. "She never said she cheated on you; she said she wasn't having sex with her therapist anymore." Jorvik frowned, while Jordan rolled his eyes. Vance looked at Dimitri and gave him a snide look. "Thanks, Dimitri…I don't know what I would do without you." Dimitri sighed and then Jorvik interjected. "You are taking this much better than the rest of us would…but you seem depressed." Vance looked at Jorvik, and then slightly looked down.

Jordan frowned, as he stared at Vance. "What, Vance?" Vance looked back up and then shrugged his shoulders. "I really don't know how to feel about this…I did the same shit to Trisha. I guess I didn't want to believe that it could happen to me. Regardless, I love my wife and I didn't get any damn sleep last night." Joron sucked his teeth. "Well, I think Jaeda cheating on me." Jordan interjected. "I know Cinco is cheating on me, and I'm just plotting my next move." Dimitri threw his hands up, as he looked between all of them. "What the hell is going on with everyone? I leave town and all of a sudden everyone is cheating again." Arianna interjected. "You mean, getting cheated on…"

Joron rolled his eyes and was disgusted. "Well, Jaeda put her cellphone on silent, and then turned it over on the nightstand." Jorvik frowned, while Vance shook his head. Jorvik looked around at everyone and then back to Joron. "And, that's it?" Arianna laughed. "That means she's doing something she has no business doing." Jorvik shot Arianna a look. "Of course, you would know that." Joron put his hand up and then dropped it. "Fuck the phone…I know whoever this dude is, he's just trying to fuck for the pregnancy pussy." The guys laughed, even Vance. Jorvik didn't know what Joron was talking about. "The what?" Arianna looked at Jorvik, and Jordan laughed. "Pregnancy pussy, Vik; one of the best types of sex there is." Dimitri frowned. "Even though that's true, how in the hell do you know?" Jordan rolled his eyes.

"I was with a few pregnant women before." Jorvik made a sarcastic sound. "That is depressing...so my brother with no children and married to a guy, has experienced pregnancy pussy? I'm the one with the kid, and don't know a damn thing of how that feels."

Dimitri shook his head. "It is a feeling you don't forget..." Jorvik interjected. "Alright, whatever...so what are you guys gonna do about your suspicions?" Vance shook his head and had no idea; Joron sighed loudly. "Y'all already know about me...I wish a nigga would try to take my damn wife." Arianna frowned, as she looked at Joron, and Jordan shook his head.

Vance stood from the couch and then sighed. "I don't know what I'm going to do...except try to call her again." Dimitri interjected. "Or maybe give her some time." Vance looked at Dimitri and then sighed; he told everyone he was leaving and told Dimitri, goodbye, before he left to head back home. Everyone told him goodbye and then afterwards, they all got back to talking.

Chapter 16

The rest of the weekend went by and it was the next day. Valerie and Dimitri were gone; Jaeda hadn't spoken to either woman since Vance and Jorvik's party. Jordan and Cinco also weren't speaking, while Joron was still suspicious of his wife. Suspicion seemed to be running ramped amongst many, of what their spouses and significant others were doing. Randy also had his concerns about his brother's outburst, at the party, towards Shavon. He had tried to call Vance, but his call was ignored. Now it was the beginning of the week again and many were trying to put themselves back together from the weekend's events.

*　　*　　*

Jaeda walked inside the barbecue place and looked around; she saw many people inside, seated, and eating. Jaeda walked in further and then walked to the counter; she slightly smiled. "Uh, I'm here to see Daniel…the owner." The woman nodded and then said she would go get him. Jaeda walked away from the counter, since she wasn't ordering food. She was about to walk to a table, when Daniel came from the back and then smiled when he saw her. He walked over to Jaeda and she turned around. "Hey, I'm glad you had time to stop by." Jaeda nodded. "Uh yeah, I'm not just here for a visit, but to talk about a job too." Daniel raised an eyebrow and then nodded; he told her to follow him and she did. Daniel walked back to his office, which was down a hall and separated from the outside area, in the back. Once in his office, he closed the door and then told her to have a seat.

Daniel sat down in his chair, behind his desk, as Jaeda sat down in the chair in front of his desk. Afterwards, Daniel slightly smiled. "Does this job change got anything to do with what happened over the weekend?" Jaeda turned her head to the side and then back to Daniel; she nodded. "Yeah, I work for Shavon and I just can't anymore after what happened. I was hoping you didn't remember what was said, but I know you do." Daniel sighed and then nodded. "It's alright, Jaeda…I…" Jaeda interjected. "I know I sounded like a hypocrite, but I just didn't cut for how Shavon treated Trisha, her man's sister-in-law. We all been through a lot over the years and I guess I'm just tired of everybody being against each other." Daniel nodded and then sighed. "Ok, well if you need a job, then you know I got you, but this is a barbecue joint, Jaeda; I know you can't cook that, so…" Jaeda interjected. "I know, Daniel, and I just need anything right now; maybe I can be a part of the waitstaff."

Daniel raised an eyebrow and then slightly laughed. "Uh, you could do that, but my girls' uniforms are not like what was going on at Hawks. I know you saw how they're dressed out there; you're pregnant too, so I don't know if I want you out there, dressed like the rest of them." Jaeda rolled her eyes. "I saw what they had on, so what are you trying to say, Daniel?" Daniel laughed and she did too; he shook his head, while he put his hands up. "I'm not saying you wouldn't look good out there in those ass shorts and tank tops, but the uniform is…" Jaeda interjected. "It's fine…I can fit the uniform, so how about it? Can I have a job, please?"

Daniel sighed and then nodded. "Yeah…and at least I get to spend time with you and see you every day, so that's a plus for me." She smiled and he did too. Daniel nodded and then stood from the chair, as she did the same. "Alright, well, I'll give you a new uniform and then you can take it home; we don't close until eleven, so you can come back in a couple of hours and I'll show you what you're gonna be doing." She nodded and then thanked him.

Daniel went over to the cabinet and then opened it to look for a uniform for her; he grabbed the right one and then walked around the desk to hand it to her. Jaeda took the hanger from him and then nodded, as he spoke. "Make sure after you start, that you let me know if something's too hard for you or if you're getting tired. I don't want you working too much, while you this far along." Jaeda nodded. "Yeah, I will." Daniel nodded and then he walked her out of his office; they walked to the front and then he watched her leave. Daniel sighed and then shook his head, before he went to check on the dining area.

Chapter 17

Jaeda returned home with her new uniform and was ready to get herself together, so she could return to Daniel's place and work. Ju was in his bedroom and playing the game, while eight-month-old Jaelyn was in her crib and asleep. Jaeda went to the master bedroom downstairs and then saw Joron asleep in the bed; she was going to be quiet and take her shower, before putting her uniform on. Jaeda went into the bathroom and then closed the door; Joron heard the door and then woke up. He rolled over in the bed and then looked around, as he yawned; he didn't work the night before and took the entire weekend off, but was still tired. Joron had the baby monitor on the nightstand, in case Jaelyn woke up, but even if he didn't hear her, he knew Ju would wake him up anyway.

Joron got out the bed and knew that Jaeda was in the shower, so he walked out the bedroom to head to the kitchen. Jaeda wasn't in the shower long and after she got out, she got herself together and then put her uniform on. Jaeda looked at herself in the mirror and then nodded; she slightly laughed as she stared at her stomach. Jaeda tried to maneuver and fit her breasts in the tank top, since they became bigger after she became pregnant. As far as she was concerned, she was just happy that the shorts fit and the tank top went over her stomach.

Jaeda exited the bathroom and then grabbed her shoes, before sitting down on the couch, and putting her shoes on. As she did this, Joron walked back into the bedroom with a bottle of water; he saw Jaeda, but not what she had on, since she was sitting. After Jaeda was finished putting her shoes on, she stood from the bed and Joron looked at her; he started to choke on his water and then coughed hysterically, as she frowned. Joron coughed hard a few more times and then got himself together. "What the fuck you got on? Where you going looking like that?" Jaeda rolled her eyes, as she walked to the dresser. "I'm going to work." Joron frowned, as he continued to stare at her. "Work, where? I know damn well Shavon don't got her people dressed like that."

Jaeda put her jewelry on and then turned around to Joron; she shook her head. "I'm not working for Shavon anymore…it's a new place, a barbecue place; this is the uniform for his girls." Joron slightly leaned his head to the side; he stared at her, as if she was crazy. "His girls? Is the owner a pimp or something?" Jaeda waved her hand around, as she walked back to the bathroom to get her cellphone; he followed her. "He's not a damn pimp, Joron; because of what happened at the party, I can't work for Shavon anymore…we're not even talking anyway."

Joron sighed and then shook his head. "Baby, you can't wear that…and in public; the damn shorts look like underwear. What type of place is this?" Jaeda turned to him and then smiled. "I'm alright, Joron; I'm fine and we talked about this already…me and the owner." Joron raised an eyebrow. "You and the owner talked about what? The only muthafucka you need to be talking to about any damn thing, is me." Jaeda frowned. "Will you calm down? It's a job, that…" Joron interjected. "That you don't need…you don't need to work. I don't care how much money we got now, you don't need to work, but I do. You on your damn feet just as much as me and trying to take care of Jaelyn and shit too. How about you slow down and stop working?" Jaeda shook her head. "I'm not doing that…now I gotta go, but I'll be back before you leave. I'll work a schedule out with Daniel."

Joron frowned. "Who the fuck is Daniel?" Jaeda sighed and decided to get this over with. "Vance and Randy's new stepbrother, Daniel." Joron stepped back from her and felt he was getting hit left and right. "Stepbrother? The dude that was at the party?" Jaeda nodded and Joron did too. "Uh huh…I didn't see y'all talk at the party, so how do you know him?" Jaeda shrugged her shoulders. "From Atlanta…we used to work together; look, I gotta go, so I'll send you a text when I get to work. Bye…love you." Jaeda quickly kissed Joron on the cheek and then left the bathroom, to leave the bedroom. Joron walked out the bathroom and then stopped in the bedroom, while wondering what just took place. He rubbed his hand down his face and then left the bedroom to go check on Jaelyn.

82

Chapter 18

Ryan was about to leave the house, when Trisha stopped him; he turned to look at her and then smiled. "Hey, I have an appointment in about an hour; I thought you were asleep and I didn't wanna wake you. Are you alright?" Trisha nodded, as she walked towards him; she stopped and then sighed. "Yeah, I'm fine; I just wanted to say again, thank you for letting me and the kids stay. I know your house is not childproof, so I'm sorry too for Vander breaking that glass." Ryan nodded and then laughed. "No problem, Trisha, and the glass can be replaced. I made a few changes to my den last night, so that's childproof now if you want the kids to play in there. And if you need to leave, then it's fine if you wanna call your nanny and have her come here." Trisha nodded and then smiled. "You have been so nice to me and I thank you." Ryan smiled and then nodded. "You're welcome, Trisha."

Ryan said he had to go and she understood; the doorbell rang and he frowned, as he turned his head. Ryan walked to the front door and then opened it. "Can I help you?" Vance stood there and stared at the man, that he saw his wife with; he clenched his jaw and had vowed not to lose his temper. "My wife is here…so let me see her." Ryan slowly nodded his head. "You're Vance, right?" Vance grit his teeth and then nodded. Ryan cleared his throat and then slightly turned his head to call for Trisha. Trisha walked to the door and then stood right next to Ryan; she saw Vance and then sighed. "Vance…what are you doing here?" Vance frowned. "What am I doing here? You left me and took my kids, so that's why I'm here. I want to see my kids, now." Ryan frowned. "I'm on my way to work, so you're not coming in this house, when I'm not here; maybe you should come back later and when you're calmed down."

Vance stepped back and then looked Ryan up and down, while taken aback how Ryan was speaking to him. "Excuse me? I don't give a fuck if you are on your way to work; this is my damn wife and my kids, so…" Trisha interjected. "Ok…it's fine; I will just leave the house for a while with the kids, so you can see them." Ryan looked at Trisha and frowned. "No, you won't, Trisha…we talked about this; stop letting him control you and bully you into doing what you don't want." Vance frowned and pushed Ryan back from Trisha, which made Ryan be pushed further back inside his house. Vance looked at Trisha. "So, you're really fucking him, huh? You're really cheating on me with this guy? You must be if he's talking like he owns you."

Ryan shot Vance a look. "Look who's talking about owning somebody…you need to leave and not ever come back to my house again." Vance stepped in Ryan's house and then got in Ryan's face. "It's taking everything I have, not to kill you with my bare hands, so telling me to leave my wife and kids, and never come back, is hazardous to your health." Ryan clenched his jaw and then Trisha interjected. "Just leave, Vance…I don't know why you are really here, but I want you to go." Vance looked at Trisha and frowned. "You don't know why I'm here? I'm here for you and the kids, that is why I'm here. I just need to talk to you and for you to talk to me." Ryan interjected. "Now you wanna talk? How many times did she try to talk to you before, and you refused to listen? How many times did you embarrass and humiliate her! Talking is not your strong suit, Vance…I'm her therapist and I know more about her, than you ever did and will. And I'm not fucking your wife, but even if I was, I think from your past indiscretions that she deserves to have another man in between her legs."

Trisha's jaw dropped, as Vance became enraged; he abruptly punched Ryan in the mouth, and made him drop his briefcase. Trisha moved out the way, as Vance went down and then continued to slam his fist into Ryan's face. Ryan got the upper hand and then head-butted Vance from off him. Vance fell to the side and then Ryan punched him back; both men were all over the floor, while Trisha yelled for them to stop.

The twins walked to the front together and then saw their daddy and Ryan fighting; they were scared and started to cry. Trisha turned her head and then went over to them. Vance elbowed Ryan in the face and that stopped the fight; Vance was breathing hard, as he stood up and then turned his head. Vance's lip was bleeding and so was the side of his head; he tried to walk over to his twins, but they cried even louder when he walked towards them. Vance stopped and then shook his head; he then looked at Trisha. "Are you happy now! My kids are scared of me!" Trisha stared at Vance, while knelt down and holding the twins. Vance wiped his mouth and then shook his head on the way out of the house. Ryan was sitting against the wall, as he breathed heavily; Trisha looked at him, as he put his head back against the wall and sighed.

Chapter 19

Shavon didn't go to work today and was at home, while sitting on the couch; she had what happened over the weekend, on her mind. The fact that Jaeda sent her a text and quit, was another blow to Shavon of how out of control everything had gotten.

Randy had walked into the living room and saw her, but didn't want to say too much to her. He tried to speak to her that night, after the party, but it didn't go too well; both argued and then Sunday, they said nothing to each other. It seemed to Randy that Shavon was depressed, but he wasn't sure whose words made the worst impact on her: Vance's or Jaeda's. Randy had to call for back up and she was on the way. The doorbell rang and Shavon ignored it; Randy walked out the living room and then to the front. He opened the door and then saw his mama; he stepped aside, so she could walk in. Afterwards, he closed the door and then looked at her. "I didn't know who else to call…she's been like a zombie all weekend and won't go to work." Lillian nodded and then said she would speak to her.

Lillian walked to the living room, but without Randy with her; he knew that both women needed to speak in private. After she reached the living room, Lillian sat down on the couch and then told Shavon to look at her. Shavon did slowly turn her head and Lillian could visibly see that Shavon had been crying and was very upset. "Randy called me over to talk to you. What is going on, Shavon?" Shavon turned her head away and then sighed; she then turned it back. "You were there, Miss Brooks…you heard what Vance said and Jaeda. Jaeda won't even talk to me and she quit working at my restaurant; she was the only friend I had in town, since Val is gone. Vance pissed at me too and probably won't ever talk to me again." Lillian sighed and then nodded. "I know what Jaeda and Vance said, were harsh, but they were right."

Shavon looked at Lillian and then shook her head; she started to protest what Lillian said, but was stopped. "Shavon, no…they were right and I just don't understand what is happening to you. I don't understand why you acted the way you did towards Trisha. I thought everything was fine and you were happy now." Shavon's lips quivered and then she shook her head; she then wiped her eyes, as she spoke. "It's not fair…" Lillian frowned, as Shavon continued. "It's not fair…that was supposed to be me, not Trisha again. I know the affair was wrong, but everybody got who they wanted except me; I know I fucked up, but I thought I had another chance…then Lily got in the way, and Trisha came back. She got what I was supposed to have with Vance; I was supposed to have his kids and be his wife." Lillian was outdone and felt she was completely wrong about what she thought was going on.

Lillian shook her head. "Shavon, I know I played a part in your decisions in the beginning, but towards the end, those were all your decisions. You decided to end your engagement to Vance, for Calvin, against my protest. And I was on your side when you decided not to be Vance's sideline anymore as well. I just assumed that after you started with Randy, that you were finally happy." Shavon shook her head. "I was, I just…I'm still in love Vance and I can't…" Lillian interjected. "Shavon, don't do this…Randy loves you and this would kill him if he found out you were still in love with Vance, and that you are obviously jealous of Trisha."

Shavon turned her head to the side and then back to Lillian. "I just don't know what to do…I gotta see Trisha when everybody gets together and I can't even stand it. I see their kids too and…" Lillian interjected. "Shavon, that is Vance's wife again…that is his family and you have to respect that; everyone has moved on and no one is a sideline anymore, not even me. You are the only one stuck in the past and it's unhealthy; you are never going to be able to move on, if you continue this hate towards Trisha and this longing to be Vance's wife. Trisha didn't do anything wrong and she tried to be your friend, but you dismissed her; she didn't have to do that. Her feelings are more fragile than yours anyway, since she sees you more and you are a reminder to her that her husband cheated on her with you."

Shavon stood from the couch, as she wiped her eyes; she then looked at Lillian. "I can't help how I feel…and I can't help that I'm still in love with Vance. I wish me and him were back together." Before either woman could speak again, someone else did. "I thought I was crazy…but it's true, huh?" Shavon and Lillian turned to see Randy standing there. Shavon put her hand over her face, as Lillian stood from the couch.

Randy walked further in the living room, as Shavon took her hand from her face; Lillian shook her head. "Randy…we…" Randy interjected. "Don't, mama…I heard everything. I was listening, because I was desperate to know what was going on. Now I gotta find out that my whole relationship with Shavon, was a lie." He looked at Shavon. "We talked about this; I asked you if you still loved Vance and you lied to my face. So, you're really jealous of Trisha, huh? You wanna be her and want Vance back, right?" Shavon crossed her arms and then slightly looked down. Randy clenched his jaw. "I can't help that you're confused, Shavon, but I know I'm not; you're gonna have to go and I guess get therapy or something to try to get over Vance."

Randy turned around to walk out the living room, when Lillian interjected. "Randy, wait…" He stopped, but didn't turn around to look at his mama. Lillian looked at Shavon and then walked over to her son; she stopped behind him. "Maybe you can take some time and think about this, before making a move based on emotions." Randy swallowed hard and then nodded.

"Fine…we'll just keep our distance for a while and act like a divorced couple sleeping in separate bedrooms." Randy said nothing else and then continued to walk out the living room.

Lillian sighed and then turned around to see Shavon staring at her. Shavon put her hand over her face and then cried hard. Lillian walked over to Shavon and then gave her a hug. "It will be alright, Shavon; just give him some time to process all this and you need to take some time, yourself." Shavon pulled back from Lillian and then nodded her head; she said she was going to lay down and Lillian thought that was a good idea. After Shavon walked out the living room, Lillian sighed and then left, while hoping that Shavon and Randy got themselves together.

Chapter 20

Joron was standing outside the barbecue place and waiting; it was lunchtime and he was waiting for his brothers. Joron took the kids to Rydell's house. He was about to lose his mind, when Jorvik and Jordan approached him; he looked between his brothers. "What the hell took y'all so long?" Jorvik frowned. "You invited us to lunch at the last damn minute and this is how you greet us?" Jordan interjected, as he looked at the establishment. "Why are we here? I don't eat barbecue." Joron rolled his eyes and then waved his hand around. "Forget all that, Jordan…eat a salad or something." Jordan frowned, as Joron turned around and told the guys to follow him inside; Joron walked in with Jordan and Jorvik behind him. The guys looked around and Jordan shook his head; they were greeted and then escorted to a table.

After the guys were seated, Jordan continued to look around, as the waitress asked what they wanted to drink. Jordan looked back at her and immediately ordered a hard drink; Jorvik looked at him and then sighed. Jorvik and Joron both ordered as well and then the waitress left the table. Jordan slightly leaned his head to the side, as he stared at the woman's ass. "Distracting uniform…the food must taste like shit, if their waitresses are walking around like that." Jorvik laughed, as Joron found nothing funny; he was there for a reason and not to check out the waitresses, as he suspected every man that dined there, did.

Joron continued to looked around and then saw who he was looking for. "There she is…" Jordan and Jorvik looked at their brother. "There who is?" The guys looked in the direction that Joron was looking in and Jordan shook his head; Jorvik frowned and then shot his brother a look. "Ron, please don't tell me you purposely brought us here. I'm not trying to get embarrassed on purpose because of you." Joron told Jorvik to keep his voice down and Jorvik threw his hands up. Jordan looked at Joron. "When did Jaeda start working here?" Joron looked at him. "Since today I guess…she came home earlier talking about she quit at Shavon's spot and working here now, at Daniel's place."

The guys frowned and Jordan spoke. "Who is Daniel?" Joron sucked his teeth. "Vance and Randy's stepbrother." Jordan and Jorvik looked at each other and then back to Joron; Jorvik shook his head. "No, Ron, hell no…I know what you're doing; don't make a damn ass out of yourself and her." Joron looked at his brother. "Why not? She used to work with that nigga in

Atlanta and I damn sure never seen them talk no other time before, so they must be talking behind my damn back. She all of a sudden putting her cellphone on silent and putting it face down on the fucking nightstand."

Jordan looked around, when Joron started to become loud; the waitress walked back over to the table and then gave the guys their drinks. She asked what they wanted to order and Joron interjected. "I need that other waitress to help us…we know her, and I wanna see the owner too." Jorvik put his hand over his face, as Jordan sighed. The waitress looked between the men and then nodded. After she walked away, Jordan shot his brother a look. "Ron, we are about to leave…I don't want to be here for whatever is about to happen." Jorvik agreed and then both men stood from their chairs; Joron stood up too. Jorvik pulled his wallet out and then took a few bills out to pay for the drinks. Joron told both of them to sit down, and then the men started to argue.

As they argued, people at other tables looked at them. Daniel and Jaeda arrived at the table and frowned. Daniel spoke. "Is there a problem?" The guys stopped and then turned their heads; Jaeda frowned, when she saw Joron and his brothers. Jordan spoke. "We don't have a problem…but I'm positive you are about to." Jorvik shook his head, as Daniel frowned; he then looked at Joron. "Joron, right? You're Jaeda's boyfriend, right?" Joron raised an eyebrow. "I'm her fucking husband, nigga." Jaeda spoke, before Daniel could. "Why are you here, Joron? Where the kids at?" Joron shot her a look. "The kids good!" Jordan sighed, as Daniel looked at Jaeda and then back to Joron; he addressed her, as he continued to stare at Joron. "I need you to tell your, uh man, to leave and then get back to work." Joron frowned. "Bitch, you can't hear…I'm her damn husband, not her man!"

Jaeda moved Daniel back and then got in front of him; she looked at Joron. "This is my job and you're making an ass out of me…go home, Joron, please." Joron looked from her and then to Daniel, who had a grin on his face. Joron swallowed hard and then shook his head. "This job or me?" Jordan and Jorvik both shot Joron a look, as he continued to stare at Daniel. Jaeda frowned. "What?" Joron gave Daniel a snide look and then looked back at Jaeda. "This job or me? This nigga or me? You don't got time to think about this shit either." Jaeda continued to frown. "Joron, you're talking stupid right now…me and Daniel not doing a damn thing, so just go home and cool off." Joron slightly leaned his head to the side. "You must be hard of hearing too…" Jordan put his hand over his face; Jorvik tried to talk some sense into his brother, but Joron didn't want to hear it.

Joron looked at Jorvik. "Nah, man…" He then looked back at Jaeda. "If I go home, then I'm getting my kids and leaving." Jaeda thought this was a joke and then crossed her arms. "Did you lose your damn mind, Joron?" Joron stepped closer to her and then got in her face. "No, but I'm about to…do you wanna see?" Daniel had enough and then pushed Joron out her face. "Get back and then get the fuck out." Joron went back forward and then punched Daniel in the face. Jorvik threw his hands up, as both guys started to fight. Many got up from their chairs and then started to take their cellphones out to record.

Jordan and Jorvik went over to break the fight up, as Jaeda moved out the way. Jorvik grabbed Daniel, as Jordan grabbed Joron; both men were pulled apart and then let go. Daniel flipped over a chair, as he stormed away from everyone. Jaeda watched him and then looked back at Joron; she shook her head. "What's wrong with you? You act like I can't have any damn male friends, or it means, I'm fucking them. I'm tired of this shit, Joron." He slowly nodded his head. "You know what I'm tired of…I'm tired of you acting like I ain't shit; like I can't take care of my own damn family. You busting your ass working, like I don't got a damn job; you just can't let me be your damn man…you did the same shit when you were pregnant with Jaelyn. You don't trust me to do shit…and now you working around that nigga that's acting like he's your damn man now. So fucking sorry that I don't own a damn business and I'm not a fucking attorney…but I'm not about to stay with a woman that looks down on me all the time. So, you can stay at your house, that your ex-husband's money paid for, but I'm going home and getting my kids…and I fucking dare you to get in my way."

Joron turned around then pushed Jaeda out the way to leave; Jorvik shook his head and then looked at Jordan. Jordan then looked at Jaeda. "Well, it was nice to see you again, Jaeda." Jordan walked away and Jorvik frowned, as he watched his brother make his way out; he then looked a Jaeda. Her eyes were red and she slightly looked around to see everyone staring at her. Jorvik sighed. "I'm not telling you to stop working here, Jaeda, but I am telling you that Ron is serious about going home and then leaving, so maybe you should leave now and go home." Jaeda shook her head.

"No, Ju's not his son, and he wouldn't take them." Jorvik sighed and then nodded; he told her, goodbye, and then walked away. Afterwards, Jaeda sighed and then walked to the office to talk to Daniel.

Chapter 21

Later that evening, Jordan had gotten off from work and went home to find his brother's car; Jordan walked in the house and heard crying, so frowned. He hung his keys on the wall and then went to the living room; he stopped and then saw Joron sitting on the couch, while rocking Jaelyn, to calm her down. Jordan dropped his briefcase by the entry of the living room and then shook his head; Cinco walked up to Jordan, as Jordan spoke. "I see you weren't playing, Ron." Cinco interjected. "No, he wasn't…" Jordan turned his head to Cinco and then looked back at his brother; he walked in the living room and then made his way over to the bar, as Cinco spoke. "I'm headed to work." Jordan made a sarcastic sound. "So early?" Cinco looked at him and then shrugged his shoulders. "Might as well…it's not like you talking to me, anyway." Cinco said nothing else, as he walked away and then left the house.

Jordan went to the bar and then looked at his brother. "I'm so happy I bought a bigger house, to accommodate you and your family." Joron gave his brother a snide look, for his sarcasm. "Whatever, Jordan…I appreciate it, bro." Jordan rolled his eyes and then took a sip of the drink, he made. "Did you talk to Jaeda?" Joron shook his head. "Hell nah…and I already know she stayed at work; I hate when people think I'm playing with them." Jordan sighed; he finished the drink he made, and then grabbed a beer from the mini fridge. "This is stupid, Ron…you just left your pregnant wife and took the kids, one that is not even yours." Joron rolled his eyes. "If I'm taking care of Ju, then he is mine. I'm just pissed all the time…and I ain't even realize what the fuck was really bothering me, until I let it all out today. I don't know if she's fucking that dude or not…but I don't even know if I care either."

Jordan shook his head. "So, what is the plan now? Are you going to live with me with your kids?" Joron sighed and then shrugged his shoulders, as he looked down at Jaelyn; she was asleep now. Joron then looked back up at his brother. "I don't know…but I know you're not gonna kick my kids out." Jordan frowned and then threw his hand up. "You're right, so just never mind, Ron; all of you can stay as long as you want." Joron sighed. "Thanks, Jordan…" Jordan nodded. Joron shook his head. "Not just for this, but…I mean, I know damn well you and Cinco don't need all this fucking space and bedrooms; y'all don't got kids and not gonna have kids." Jordan raised an eyebrow, as he stared at his brother. "So, what are you getting at?"

Joron slightly smiled. "You still trying to take care of all of us…whenever I need a spot to stay, Vik, Arianna, any of us, the kids…we're always welcome to stay with you."

Jordan slightly grinned. "Uh huh…well, I don't cook, so don't ask; which bedroom is Ju in?" Joron slightly laughed and then nodded. "I got Jaelyn in the bedroom with me, in her portable playpen, and Ju in the one down the hall from us. We all upstairs, and nowhere near the master down here, or the other guest bedroom." Jordan nodded and then smiled; he said he was going to take a shower and then go to the club later. Joron nodded and then after Jordan left the living room, Joron got up from the couch and then took Jaelyn to the bedroom.

Chapter 22

Later that night, Dean was behind the bar and glancing at Cinco off and on; Cinco caught him and then slightly laughed, as he made his way over to him. Cinco shook his head. "I don't see how you can do your damn job, if you keep staring at me all night." Dean laughed and then nodded. "I'm trying my best not to stare, but I can't help it; it's not too busy tonight, so how about we slip away to your office?" Cinco turned his head away and then shook it. "I can't do this again…I needed it the first time, but…" Dean interjected. "Come on, Cinco…you still need it. Your man probably too distracted with the thoughts of the dead previous owner, so while we're at work, we can accommodate each other…make each other feel good." Dean licked his lips, as he stared at Cinco.

Cinco turned his head back to him and then sighed, as he eyed him. Cinco looked around and then back to Dean; he nodded his head and then walked away. Dean smiled and also looked around, as both men left from behind the bar, and then went to the office. Once in the office, Dean closed the door and then both men turned to each other; they started to kiss and then remove their shirts, in between kisses. They made their way to the couch and then Cinco got on top of Dean, while he laid back on the couch; they started to undo each other's jeans and then Dean slightly pulled Cinco's jeans and underwear down.

They continued kissing and then the office door opened. Jordan walked in and then frowned. "What the fuck!" Cinco and Dean immediately stopped; Cinco almost fell off the couch, while trying to get up from on top of Dean. Cinco stood up and then Dean sat up on the couch, but didn't stand. Jordan kept his eyes on Cinco and then turned his head to Dean; he did a doubletake. "What the fuck is this?" He looked back at Cinco, as he tried to speak. "Jordan, look this just happened…it's not what you think." Jordan looked Cinco up and down. "Do I look like a fucking amateur? I know what this is, but you go and fuck my ex? Is this your way of getting back at me, for being bitter over Tyler?" Cinco frowned. "Your ex? What the hell are you talking about? Dean is your ex?" Jordan frowned. "Who the fuck is Dean?"

Dean stood from the couch and then shook his head, as Cinco looked at him. "This guy is Dean." Jordan didn't know what was going on, but was about to find out; he also looked at Dean. "What the hell are you trying to pull, Les?" Cinco's eyes grew big. "Les?

Les, like in Leslie…like in Amber and Leslie? He said his name was Dean." Leslie looked between the men and then started to zip his jeans up; he looked from Cinco and then to Jordan. "It's good to see you again, Jordan…I knew this was gonna be easy; it was too easy and I felt like I was working undercover again." Jordan shook his head and then looked at Cinco, who still had a confused look on his face. "Well Cinco, it looks like you were played." Cinco looked back at him.

Leslie slightly laughed and then nodded, as Jordan looked back at him. Leslie looked at Cinco. "Your cousin Nick, is with my ex-husband, Terry now…Nick spilled the beans to the wrong person about Jordan's new man and husband. Terry is using Nick, just like Jordan used me." Jordan frowned, as he stared at Leslie. "I never used you…" Leslie made a sarcastic sound, as he looked at Jordan. "Yeah, you did, Jordan…like you use everybody; but I never thought you'd do it to me. I know I made a mistake but you ended it with me and just stopped talking to me, without no damn explanation. So, the way I see it, yeah, you used me. So, I decided payback was the only way I was gonna feel better after you dropped me, for Nick, and then for Cinco. And it wasn't hard either, Jordan…Cinco never mentioned he was married to you or even mentioned your name to me; you were just some dude…his words, not mine."

Jordan looked at Cinco and then clenched his jaw, as Leslie continued. "The sex was alright…nothing how it was with you, Jordan…but I did recognize some of your moves; and when I fucked him, I thought about you, so that should make you feel better." Jordan looked back at Leslie and then slowly nodded his head.

Cinco interjected. "Jordan…this dude set me up. I wasn't even thinking about cheating with anybody; he came to me and starting talking about Tyler and…" Jordan interjected. "Shut the fuck up!" Cinco closed his mouth and Leslie shook his head.

Jordan sarcastically laughed. "A damn setup? Yeah, it was a setup, Cinco, but it wasn't a brilliant one; his middle name is Dean…did he even fill out an application or did you just verbally hire him with no paperwork? Did you do a background check or anything?" Cinco turned his head away and Jordan received his answer. Jordan then looked at Leslie. "I should really beat your ass, Les…but I never had someone go through so much trouble to get back at me, for anything…especially when they are still in love with me." Leslie slightly turned his head and then cleared his throat, as Cinco looked at him. "So, you're still in love with him too? This whole damn thing was to break us up, and for what? You thought he was gonna run back into your damn arms!"

Jordan raised an eyebrow and continued to watch the guys go back and forth. Leslie frowned, as he looked at Cinco. "You don't know shit about Jordan, do you? I got a better chance of being back in his bed now, than you…you cheated on him, not me. I never cheated on Jordan and he knows that. I was what he wanted…not Amber, not Tyler, not Nick, and damn sure not you." Cinco stared at Leslie and had no words to say to that. Leslie grinned. "It looks like you fucked up, Cinco…" Leslie started to laugh and then walked away from him; he glanced at Jordan, and the glance was returned.

When Leslie reached the door, he turned around to the guys. "And uh, by the way…I quit." Leslie laughed again, as he turned around and then walked out the office. After he was gone, Jordan looked back at Cinco, who finally looked back at him. "Jordan…I'm sorry; I was good until he…well, he came at me first and I wasn't even interested in him." Jordan walked over to Cinco and then stopped. "He came at you, because you let him; you hired someone that had no experience bartending and I know that for a fact, because I know where he works. You didn't ask him shit, you just looked at him and he was hired on the spot, with minimal paperwork filled out or maybe he did fill out paperwork, but something distracted you from paying attention to it. Then he fed you bullshit lies about Tyler and my love for him, when it wasn't true. I don't talk about Tyler for a reason and it has nothing to do with still being in love with him. It has to do with guilt…for him taking his life and leaving me his club, his prized possession. Guilt is what I feel, not love, so that is the reason I don't come here a lot. Les was right, because you fucked up…you fucked up our marriage and what we had; you stopped wanting sex with me, it wasn't the other way around. If I would have known that you were going to cheat, I would have been cheated with someone else already."

Cinco slightly nodded his head. "So, that's it? It was a mistake, so what are you talking about doing now?" Jordan made a sarcastic sound. "Maybe you should go visit your cousin Nick for a while; maybe ask him and Terry if you can stay with them, until you get back on your feet." Jordan turned around and then walked away; Cinco stopped him. "You're kicking me

out, just like that? We can't even talk about this?"
Jordan stopped at the door, but didn't turn around, as
he spoke. "I recall you telling me something about
taking a walk…so walk, Cinco." Jordan continued out
the office and Cinco put his hand over his face; he
dropped it and then hit his fist on the desk. Cinco
zipped his jeans and then walked out the office too.

Chapter 23

Jordan returned home and found extra vehicles parked outside his house; he frowned, as he walked in his house. Jordan walked to his living room and then found Vance, Joron, Arianna and Jorvik. Jordan looked between all of them with a frown still on his face. "What the hell?" Everyone turned to look at him. Arianna waved. "Hey, Jordan…" Jorvik laughed, as Jordan rolled his eyes. "I'm happy everyone is comfortable…does anybody need another drink?" Vance slightly laughed at Jordan's sarcasm. "I'm good." Jordan sighed and then threw his keys on the end table. "Ron, I need you to work tonight…before Cinco blows up my damn club." They all looked at him and frowned.

Joron looked at him. "I'm off tonight and who gonna watch my kids?" Jordan gave him a snide look. "I hope you didn't think I was going to watch your kids at night, while you work? Ju is old enough to watch himself, but you have a baby." Joron threw his hands up and then looked at Jorvik. "What about you…y'all got a nanny and shit, so can she watch Jaelyn?" Arianna raised an eyebrow, as Jorvik frowned. Arianna spoke. "Where is your wife and why can't she watch her kids?" Jorvik cleared his throat, while Vance and Arianna were confused. Jordan frowned. "You didn't tell them?" Vance spoke. "Tell us, what?"

Jorvik made a sarcastic sound. "Ron left his wife and took the kids with him." Vance and Arianna looked at Joron; Arianna was confused. "Ju is not even your son, so you just took him too and left? I'm surprised she didn't call the cops on you." Vance laughed, as Jordan did too; Jorvik shook his head, while Joron gave them all a snide look. "I wasn't about to leave him; this shit just happened today and I thought I was off tonight, so I didn't have time to get a damn babysitter for overnight. And why the hell I gotta go in anyway, if Cinco there? He's the damn manager."

Jordan sighed and then shook his head. "I caught him cheating…in the act. I said a lot, but the one thing I forgot to tell him, before I left, was that he was fired." Vance shook his head, as Arianna made a sarcastic sound. "Oh wow, I see everyone has lost their damn mind. Who was he with?" Jordan looked at Arianna. "The new bartender, uh, Dean…" Arianna frowned, as Joron shook his head. "I knew something was going on between them niggas." Jordan put his hand up and then dropped it; he stood from the bar stool and then looked around at everyone. "I'm going to bed…so what are you going to do, Ron?" Joron threw his hands up. "Jordan, I can't leave my baby with you, especially if you not gonna watch her; she usually sleeps all night, but sometimes she wakes up."

Arianna rolled her eyes and then stood from the couch. "Alright, enough of all this…me and Vik are staying the night with Evan; we'll take your bedroom and put Evan and Jaelyn in her playpen. Ju has his own room and when you get off in the morning, you can take the bedroom downstairs, until we wake up. Vance might as well stay the night and take the other guest bedroom, by the game room." Jordan frowned, the entire time she spoke. "Excuse me, Arianna, but is this your house, or mine, because right now I can't tell? Is it alright if I go to my bedroom now? Is it still the place I'm sleeping tonight?" Arianna gave Jordan a snide look and Vance laughed with the guys. Jordan put his hands up and then dropped them; he told everyone goodnight and then went to bed. Jaelyn and Evan were playing on the floor, so both were picked up and then taken upstairs. Afterwards, everyone was situated for the night and then Joron left for work.

Chapter 24

One month later…

Much had occurred from the previous month; Jaeda went home that night to find that Joron had left with Ju and Jaelyn. She tried to call him, but he didn't answer. Jaeda called Ju and he told her that they were alright and at Uncle Jordan's house. Jaeda didn't attempt to call Joron again, but did keep in touch with Ju and asked about Jaelyn. Jaeda continued to work at Daniel's barbecue place, while giving her and Joron some space. Randy and Shavon were no longer together; he wanted her to move out and she did. Randy couldn't get past everything he heard and found out, in regards to how Shavon truly felt.

Vance and Trisha hadn't spoken again, but Vance did leave Trisha voicemails; the twins' first birthday had passed and Vance went to Ryan's house to give his gifts to his kids. That was the last time he saw his kids. Once again, more time and space were given to accommodate those who needed it. Jordan and Cinco were different from everyone else; it didn't seem to faze Jordan as much as everyone had thought. Cinco also still lived at the house with Jordan, even though he was originally kicked out; they slept in separate bedrooms and were still married. Cinco was also still working at the club and managing it, while everyone was dumbfounded, that he still had his job. Joron found it disturbing and hard to work with Cinco, while knowing what he did. Jordan had to explain to his brother that if he wanted to be home at night for the kids, then Cinco had to stay at the club to open and close. In the midst of all this, Shavon and Jaeda still weren't speaking, but Valerie did speak to Shavon, just not to Jaeda.

*   *   *

Vance was about to leave the house; he opened the door and then almost ran into Randy. "Hey, what's going on?" Randy saw that Vance was dressed, so assumed that he was on his way out. "Uh, hey, this won't take long. Can I talk to you?" Vance nodded and then Randy walked away from the door. Vance stepped outside and then locked up; he then walked over to Randy. "So, what's going on?" Randy stood there with his hands in his pockets and then sighed. "I broke up with Shavon and she moved out." Vance was surprised to hear that. "I didn't know that. I'm sorry, Randy." Randy nodded and then shrugged his shoulders. "I was trying to make myself believe that I could make Shavon happy, but I couldn't." Vance nodded. "It's not your fault, Randy; maybe you two just weren't compatible."

Randy thought that was an understatement and then sarcastically laughed. "Well, she's never gonna be compatible with anybody, because she's still in love with you." Vance frowned and then shook his head. "Come on, Randy, that is over and done with; I moved on with Trisha. Trisha left me and took the kids, but I'm still trying to get her back. I don't want anyone but her." Randy slowly nodded his head and then cleared his throat. "I heard mama and Shavon talking…so yeah, you moved on, but she hasn't. Shavon hates Trisha because she's your wife again, and not Shavon; she wants you back. That's the reason for Shavon treating Trisha like that. I got an earful, but I just wanted to let you know, just in case Shavon comes to you and tries to fuck up what you and Trisha got going on. I won't tell her that Trisha left you, because I know that's something she wants to happen, so she can slide back in your life."

Vance was dumbfounded and had no idea. He hadn't thought about Shavon again, since he and Trisha got married and started a family; especially after he confronted Shavon at his birthday party. Vance hated that Randy was obviously used and put in the middle of this. "Damn, Randy, I'm so sorry…I don't even know what to say." Randy shook his head. "I don't know what to say either, except I think I moved too fast with Shavon. Anyway, it's a damn lesson learned, and I'm single again; thirty-nine years old and single again." Randy shook his head, as Vance slightly laughed. "That's right, thirty-nine…your birthday was a few days ago, right?" Randy looked at Vance and nodded.

Vance sighed. "I forgot, I'm sorry…but hey, I'm on my way out to Jordan's club; he invited all of us to just have fun tonight, so come with me." Randy shook his head. "I don't know, man." Vance interjected. "Come on, we all have so much going on and I need this as much as you probably do." Randy nodded and agreed to go; Vance nodded and then the guys left in Vance's car to head to the club.

Chapter 25

Arianna was at Jordan's club, along with Jordan, Vance, Randy, Jorvik, Joron, and even Dimitri was there; he was in town, but without Valerie and the kids. Everyone was taking shots and having a good time, while standing and sitting around a high bar table. Jordan was on shot number three already. Joron frowned. "Damn, man…how many more you gonna take?" Jordan looked at his brother and frowned. "I'm just trying to have a good time…now I am about to go dance." Jorvik raised an eyebrow. "You? You are going to dance?" They all looked at Jorvik and Arianna laughed. "You didn't know that Jordan could dance?" She looked at Jordan. "Go show them how it's done, baby." Jorvik looked at her and frowned, as Dimitri and the others laughed.

Randy shook his head and then swallowed down his shot. "Well, I see a woman over there that has my name on her, so if y'all will excuse me." Randy walked away from the table, as Vance shook his head. A waitress brought more drinks to the table and then took the empty glasses with her. Afterwards, Arianna started to move with Jorvik holding her from behind. Dimitri looked out and then squinted his eyes. "I see Jordan bounced back fast from Cinco." They all turned their heads and looked out, to see Jordan on the dance floor. Joron shook his head. "That's a damn shame…Jordan fucking with the dude that Cinco cheated on him with." Everyone shot him a look and frowned.

Dimitri raised an eyebrow. "Cinco cheated on Jordan with Les?" Joron frowned. "Who's Les? I'm talking about that dude grinding on Jordan right now." Vance nodded. "That is Leslie, Jordan's ex…" Joron looked around at everyone and then shook his head. "No, that's Dean…the dude that Cinco hired; he was the one that I said was too close to Cinco." Jorvik frowned, as Dimitri put his hand over his face. Arianna's jaw dropped and then she slapped her hand down on the table. "Oh, that is fucking classic…Dean is Leslie's middle name, but he must have pulled the ultimate "I'm going to get my man back" plot." They all frowned, as they looked at her.

Joron was confused. "What the hell you talking about?" Arianna sighed. "Les never got over Jordan…and Jordan told me that this Dean guy lied about his bartending experience just to get the job here, and then played Cinco for a fool, to break him and Jordan up. Jordan never told me it was Les…and I see why now. Bravo to Les for taking back what was his."

They all frowned once again and Jorvik shook his head at her. "Bravo to Les, huh? Well, did you give Ethan a standing ovation for taking back what was his, by blackmailing you three damn times? Or were you waiting for one of us to do it?" Arianna gave Jorvik a snide look and then elbowed him in the stomach. Vance laughed and Dimitri cleared his throat.

Dimitri stared out at the guys. "I don't even know if you can call what they are doing, dancing. I don't even want to see that anymore." Dimitri turned his head and Arianna laughed, when she looked out at them and saw. Jorvik rolled his eyes and then Joron swallowed down his drink; he was about to leave the table, when Jorvik stopped him. "Where the hell are you going?" Joron frowned, as he looked at his brother. "I'm about to go dance." Jorvik shook his head. "With who?" Vance frowned, as Dimitri shook his head. Joron continued to frown. "Damn, Vik, do I need your permission to dance?" Jorvik quickly nodded his head. "Yes, you do…my fighting days at a club out with you, are over. That's why I stopped going out with you in Dallas; I don't have time to have your back all night. You can't dance anyway, so why even embarrass yourself by going out there." The guys laughed, as Joron rolled his eyes.

Vance looked at Jorvik. "He's your brother, so you're supposed to have his damn back." Jorvik shot him a look. "If someone is fucking with Ron, then yes, but that's not ever the case…Ron is always caught on the dance floor with another man's bitch; that's how the fights always start. But then again, the way Ron dances, it looks like he's having a seizure so, maybe that misunderstanding is how the fights always start."

Dimitri laughed hard, as Vance followed his lead. Joron rolled his eyes and Arianna interjected. "Vik, you're overreacting…I think it's sexy to watch men fight."

Vance put his hand over his face and laughed, as Jorvik looked her up and down. "Baby, I'll accommodate any fetish you have, but if getting elbowed in the throat is a turn on for you, then you're going to have to find another way to get off." Arianna frowned, as the guys laughed hard. Joron continued to laugh, but they all stopped when Cinco walked over; they all looked at him. "I know Jordan is here; I saw him at the table with y'all earlier, so where is he?" Joron looked around at everyone and then cleared his throat. "I don't know, I ain't his keeper." Dimitri frowned, as Vance shook his head. Arianna rolled her eyes and then sighed. "On the dance floor, Cinco." He looked at her and then looked out. Cinco looked around and then spotted Jordan; he saw Jordan with his arms around Leslie from behind, while Leslie moved against him.

Cinco slowly nodded his head and then reached in his back pocket to pull something out. Arianna looked around at the guys and then back to Cinco, when they all saw Cinco slide the brass knuckles on his hand. Joron frowned. "Who the fuck you using that on?" Cinco looked at Joron with a blank expression on his face. "Jordan is still my damn husband…" Cinco walked away from the table and Jorvik threw his hands up. "It never fails…" He looked at Arianna. "I guess you are going to get off, after all." Arianna frowned; Dimitri put his hand over his face and Vance laughed. Vance put his hand up. "Hold on, that's not for Jordan…I think that's for Leslie." They all turned their heads, and then all hell broke loose.

Chapter 26

Cinco made his way onto the dance floor and then over to Jordan and Leslie; he reached them and then pushed Jordan back from Leslie. Leslie turned around and then frowned, when he saw Cinco; he then slightly grinned. "What's going on, Cinco?" Cinco looked at Jordan. "So, you back with him, now?" Jordan frowned, as he looked Cinco up and down. "I'm not back with anyone…I'm just having fun tonight. It doesn't look like you're having fun, Cinco." Leslie slightly laughed, as Cinco stared at Jordan. "You kept me working here, you let me stay at the house, but you're ignoring me and fucking other dudes; you're trying to play me, like this dude did?" Jordan rolled his eyes. "I didn't keep you any damn where…I think I've been pretty good to you, considering you are the one that cheated on me. You still have your job, a place to live, and me out your face…so that is a good deal. We are still married, Cinco, so whether I want to or not, I'm still taking care of your ass."

Cinco clenched his jaw and Leslie had enough. "Jordan, can we get back to what we were doing?" Cinco turned around to him and then frowned. "Hell no…" Leslie was about to speak again, when Cinco punched him in the face; Leslie fell back into someone else, and before anyone could get their balance, Cinco went back to Leslie and punched him again with the brass knuckles on. Jordan stood there and then rolled his eyes, as both Leslie and Cinco fought. More men got involved when they were either bumped or pushed by the brawling men. More bumps and pushes took place and then fists started to fly amongst more people than just Cinco and Leslie. Randy was one of the men that started fighting when he was pushed by another guy, on accident. Vance had already jumped into the brawl and Jordan walked away.

Jordan walked back to the table and then Dimitri, Joron, Arianna, and Jorvik looked at him. Jordan sat down on the high stool and then lit a cigarette; he then saw everyone staring at him. "What?" Dimitri laughed and Joron shook his head. Jorvik was outdone. "You started all that and need to get your ass beaten with the rest of them." Arianna laughed, as Jordan waved his hand around. "I didn't start anything…Cinco started that. Someone will break it up." Joron frowned. "Nigga, this is your club, you supposed to break it up. I told you, you were drinking too much." Jordan rolled his eyes; he took his cellphone off his hip and then called his security out front, to come inside. Shortly after, many security officers ran inside and then started to regulate the fights taking place.

Vance and Randy stopped on their own, after Vance pulled Randy away from someone; they made their way to the table and once there, everyone looked at them. Dimitri shook his head. "Wow…" Randy rolled his eyes and then grabbed a napkin off the table to wipe the blood from his mouth. Vance shook his head and then swallowed down his drink. "Well, I think I released all my anger and frustration out tonight." Arianna shook her head, as Jordan looked at them. "I have some bandages in my office, so I'll get them for you, Randy." Vance looked at him. "I think that's the least you can do, Jordan, since you started that fight." Jordan put his hand up. "Whatever, Cinco started it." Arianna interjected. "I can't believe you just let them fight." Jordan frowned, as he looked at her. "I should have beaten both of their asses when I caught them on the couch in my damn office, but I didn't; so, hell no, I wasn't stopping them. I'm going to get those bandages." Jordan got off the stool and then walked away, to go to his office.

Not too long after, Cinco walked over and they all looked at him. "Where did Jordan go?" Joron rolled his eyes. "He's coming back, so just wait like the rest of us." Cinco gave Joron a snide look, but said nothing else. Shortly after, Jordan returned to the table and then saw Cinco; he ignored him, as he handed the bandages and gauze to Randy. Cinco looked at Jordan. "We need to talk…" Jordan looked at him and then shook his head, no. "I didn't come out to talk…I came to relax; how is Les doing?" They all looked from Jordan and then to Cinco. Cinco swallowed hard. "I don't know, the last I saw, security was dragging his ass out the club." Jordan nodded. "Alright, well get back to work." Cinco sighed and then nodded, before walking away from the table.

Jordan watched him and then got back to his drink and cigarette. Dimitri shook his head. "You don't really care." Jordan frowned, as he looked at Dimitri. "I don't care about what?" Dimitri slightly leaned his head to the side. "You don't care that he cheated. I know what you are doing, Jordan, and I'm not trying to sound like a hypocrite, but you are wrong." Vance looked at Dimitri and then back to Jordan, as he addressed Dimitri. "And what is he doing? I think the blow to the head made my comprehension a little slower." Arianna and Jorvik laughed, as Dimitri shook his head. "He's punishing Cinco…basically torturing him, daily." Joron frowned and was still confused, but more so because he wasn't in his brother's business.

Jordan looked at Dimitri. "I don't know what you're talking about." Dimitri rolled his eyes and Jorvik intervened. "Come on, Jordan…if you didn't want Cinco, then you would have kicked him out the house already and fired him. You know, you want him around and still love him." Jordan blew smoke out his nose and then put his cigarette out in the ashtray on the table. "And…what if I am punishing him? He deserves it…he cheated on me." Arianna sighed. "Les played him for a damn fool, Jordan; you remember how you and Les met, right? I asked him to play your man, to make Tyler jealous and it worked so good, that Les blew the whistle on the plot, because he fell for you." Jorvik frowned, as he looked at Arianna. "You asked that guy to do that? So, you really started this." Jordan laughed and so did the others; Arianna rolled her eyes and then got back to Jordan. "Anyway, you can't knock Les for going undercover again and trying. I mean, I had no idea he was doing this…he still works at the magazine during the day. I just saw him today."

Vance rolled his eyes and Dimitri shook head. "I think it's obvious that Les still wants Jordan back, but you need to choose." Arianna interjected again. "It's more than just choosing…you should have talked to Les instead of ending it with him, and then ignoring him for what…two years. I would be mad too if someone did that to me with no explanation." Jordan threw his hands up and then nodded; Randy looked at his watch and then back up again. "Vance, I'ma head out; thanks for tonight, but I need some pain pills and my bed." Vance laughed and then nodded; he felt the same. "Alright, well we rode together, so I'm going to head out too. I'll talk to you all tomorrow."

Dimitri and Vance slapped hands and then everyone told the guys, goodbye. After they left, Jorvik said they should get home and relieve the nanny; Joron was going with them to pick up Ju and Jaelyn from their house. Everyone made their way out and then Dimitri looked at Jordan. "Are you ready?" Jordan looked at him and then nodded. Dimitri was staying with Jordan for the weekend, so they rode together. Jordan told Dimitri that he would meet him outside; Dimitri nodded and then left, as Jordan walked over to the bar.

When Jordan reached the bar, Cinco looked up at him. Jordan sighed. "When you get off in the morning, come to my room and wake me up, so we can talk."

Jordan said nothing else, but turned around, and then walked away from the bar. Cinco watched him and then sighed, as he got back to work.

Chapter 27

It was the next day, very early in the morning; Cinco had closed the club and didn't bother cleaning up, as he usually would. He decided to clean up after he opened again that night. Cinco knew that Jordan had a house full, so he was quiet when he walked in the house. Cinco went to take his shower first, since he was bruised from the brawl he was in with Leslie. After his shower, he went to the master bedroom and then slowly opened the door; he closed it behind him and then walked over to the bed. Cinco saw Jordan asleep, so he got in the bed and then sat against the headboard; Cinco didn't wake up Jordan, as he was told, but just sat there.

It was twenty minutes later, when Jordan attempted to roll over and felt a body; he opened his eyes and then saw Cinco sitting on the bed. Jordan shifted and then slightly rose; he looked at the time and then back to Cinco. "How long have you been here?" Cinco turned his head to Jordan. "Awhile…I just wanted to sit here next to you, before I woke you up, because I know you're gonna kick me out after." Jordan sat all the way up and then leaned against the headboard as Cinco was. "Alright…I'm up now anyway. So, what was the issue last night, with Les?" Cinco frowned and then shot Jordan a look. "What? The issue was him fucking with you…" Jordan interjected. "We're not fucking…Les is smart and knows what he's doing to get under your skin, but…" Cinco interjected. "Does anybody ever get over you? Does anybody ever stop loving you? I hadn't met an ex of yours yet, that don't want you back."

Jordan turned his head straight and then sighed; he shrugged his shoulders. "Tyler committed suicide…and yes, he left me his club. He was my sideline and I loved him, but not enough to come out for him, or end my marriage to Mya. I finally did come out, but it wasn't for him; I just felt it was time for me. Anyways, I'm not sure what happened, but Tyler took a break from me and I assumed it was over, so I started with Amber and Les; we were in a three-way relationship. Regardless, when I wanted it to be over, then it was over."

Cinco slightly nodded his head, as he listened and then sighed. "Yeah, I remember you telling me something like that…so, you're not still in love with Tyler or anybody else?" Jordan turned his head to Cinco. "No…" Cinco nodded and then Jordan spoke again, before Cinco could. "Look Cinco, if you cheated on me with a stranger then I would have been mad, but since it was Les and I know what he did to you, is why I'm not mad." Cinco frowned and was confused. "If you don't care, then why you been ignoring me and throwing that dude in my face, at the club? I said I was sorry and…" Jordan interjected. "I know, Cinco…I was just punishing you, for what you did, but maybe I went a little too far. I didn't realize you were going to strap up with brass knuckles and almost beat Les to death." Cinco looked down and then slightly laughed; he then looked back up again at Jordan, who slightly laughed too. Cinco nodded. "I love you…I do and I'm sorry; and whether you know it or not, last night wasn't gonna be the only night I went after that guy. As long as I'm still married to you, then whoever you tried to be with, was gonna get the same treatment."

Jordan looked at him and then shook his head, as he sighed. "I said I went too far; I acknowledged that and that was it, with me playing games by using Les." Cinco nodded. "Alright, so I need to know what happens now." Jordan rubbed his hands down his face and then nodded; he then put his head back against the headboard, as Cinco stared at him. "I love you, Cinco…I would have gotten rid of you already if I didn't." Cinco frowned. "Is that shit supposed to make me feel better, Jordan?" Jordan turned his head to him. "I love you, so we'll get past this and move on…I'm not mad about any of this anymore, and the only solution I give a damn about is anything that involves me getting laid. I haven't had sex in close to three months…so I'm frustrated."

Cinco slightly laughed and then nodded. "Ok, how about I quit being the manager of the club? I'll go back to just bartending and make my own schedule, so that I'm home at night to take care of my man." Jordan eyed him and then nodded. "That's a start…" Cinco nodded and then leaned in to kiss Jordan; it became deeper and then Jordan laid back, so Cinco could get all the way on top of them. It was long overdue for Jordan, and Cinco was willing to do whatever it took, to make it up to him.

Chapter 28

It was the next day and Vance woke up to pain from the night before; he thought he only had a few bruises and war wounds, but after he fully went to sleep and then woke up, he felt the aftermath of his actions the next day. Vance got himself together in the bathroom and then walked out to hear his doorbell ring; he walked out his bedroom and then to the front. Vance opened the door and then saw Shavon; she nodded. "Hey Vance, can we talk?" He nodded and then stepped aside, so she could walk in; he closed the door after and they both walked to the living room.

Once in there, they both sat down on the couch and Shavon looked around, before looking back at him. "Is Trisha here?" Vance sighed and then shook his head. "No…" Shavon nodded. "Alright, well, I gotta talk to you about what happened at your party." Vance didn't want to listen to Shavon, but decided to hear her out anyway. "I know I was wrong and everything you said was right. I just…well, I still love you and I never stopped; I know I said I wasn't trying to get you back in my life, but I really was. The whole restaurant thing, was to get you back; I mean, I did want my own restaurant again, but I came to you."

Vance nodded, as she continued. "I wanna know if you still feel anything for me, because if you do, then I'll leave Randy." Vance frowned and then turned his head to the side, before looking back at her. "You will leave Randy? You will break up with Randy, if I said I still what, love you and want you?" Shavon nodded and Vance had to stop this now; he abruptly stood from the couch and she looked up at him. "Uh Shavon, Randy is my brother, in case you forgot; he already told me that he broke up with you, because he heard you and my mama talking." Shavon stood from the couch and slightly had her mouth open; it seemed to Vance as if she was trying to come up with another lie to tell. He shook his head. "Don't, Shavon…I don't love you and I don't want you. I wasn't going to tell you this, but I will; Trisha left me and took my kids. They've been gone for a month now. She left because she was sick and tired of being treated like a damn outsider and not my wife. But that's my fault, for thinking that you would ever treat her like that. I'm not oblivious to what was happening anymore."

Shavon tried to speak and Vance told her to shut up; he was getting angrier with every word that had already came out of her mouth. "Right now, is the very last time that I will ever see you; Randy broke up with you, so there is no reason for you to be around me, him, or our family anymore. And if by chance Randy did take you back, then me and my family won't come around, unless Randy is alone. I wish you well with your restaurant and your future, but I need for you to go…now." Shavon swallowed hard and then wiped her cheeks, when she felt tears roll down them. She nodded and then turned around to leave; he followed her to make sure she left.

After they reached the door, Vance opened it and Trisha was standing there; she was about to ring the doorbell. Trisha saw Shavon and then cleared her throat. "I'm sorry, I can come back another time." Vance frowned. "The hell you are." He reached out and then grabbed Trisha's hand to pull her inside the house. Shavon looked at them, as Trisha looked at Vance, and then back at Shavon. Shavon said nothing, as she turned around and then left.

Afterwards, Vance closed the door and then looked at Trisha. "Hey…I didn't know you were coming by." Trisha slowly nodded her head. "Since Shavon was here, I believe it." Vance sighed, as he took her hand. "She came over here on her own; I didn't call her. She wanted to talk and I let her talk; I also had some words for her too. The point I'm trying to make is that I told Shavon to her face, that I don't want her or love her; I love you and she is permanently out of our lives for good." Trisha slightly nodded her head and then took her hand from Vance; she walked around him to walk to the living room. Vance turned around and followed her.

Chapter 29

Once in the living room, Trisha sat down on the couch and then crossed her legs; Vance followed her lead. Trisha sighed. "I had a lot of time to think…and I just…I'm tired of being walked on by everyone. I don't want my kids to grow up seeing me depressed and crying all the time. I don't want them to think I'm weak either." Vance swallowed hard and then nodded. "Ok…so, what does that mean? Are you not coming back home?" Trisha looked down and then back up again at him; she shook her head. "No, Vance…" Vance slightly nodded his head, as he looked away; he sighed and then became emotional with the thought of not seeing his kids every day again.

Vance cleared his throat and then looked back at Trisha. "So, do you want a divorce? Is that where this is leading to?" Trisha paused for a moment, before she spoke again. "Why did you cheat on me with Shavon?" Vance stared at her and then slightly opened his mouth. "Trisha, don't do this...please." She shook her head. "We never spoke about this and I think I have the right to know why my husband didn't want me anymore." Vance felt this was one way to ensure that Trisha left him for good and never returned, but would answer her questions.

Vance sighed. "Alright, well, at the time...I want to make that clear right now, Trisha, at the time and not now...I thought you were stuck-up and high maintenance. I thought your attitude was horrible, since you made others feel like they were beneath you. In the bedroom, you wouldn't let loose and had too many negative things to say about what you couldn't do and didn't want to do, like I was a stranger off the streets and not your husband. You didn't want children either, and I did; you kept going on about how much my mama hated you, but you hated her too. You just weren't fun to be around and I dreaded going out in public with you, but did anyway for appearance purposes."

Trisha took a deep breath and soaked in everything that Vance just said to her; a lot of it actually hurt, but she asked the question. "And all of that, was the opposite of Shavon, right?" Vance nodded his head and she did too. "So, why did you marry me in the first place?" Vance sat back against the couch and then rubbed his hands down his face. "Because I didn't know...I didn't know what I was getting into, with you.

By that time, it was too late…so, I just decided to keep being married to you, while cheating on you with Shavon." Trisha nodded and then discreetly wiped her eyes; Vance turned his head to her and then shook it. "Baby, this is why I didn't want to do this…please don't cry. I'm sorry…I'm so sorry, baby."

Trisha put her hand up to stop him and then dropped it; she cleared her throat. "I get it and I understand…since you were truthful with me, is why I'm going to be truthful with you. Ryan is my former therapist; after our divorce, I started seeing him. He knows all about you and our marriage the first time around; he knows how I felt and every session, I cried. We started having sex, then he told me he was married; I ended it that day and never went back to him, until recently, because I needed my therapist again." Vance listened and then nodded, as he looked down. Trisha told Vance to look at her and he did. "He is divorced now, but the point is, I ended it because when he told me he was married, I instantly felt guilt. His wife was me…I was his wife. I couldn't do to another woman, what was done to me, no matter how I felt. And even with everything that you put me through in our marriage, I still couldn't bring myself to cheat on you or anyone I was with. Ryan kissed me and he tried to go further, but I stopped him; we haven't been having sex."

Vance didn't know what to feel or what to say; he was told a lot and was trying to process everything, while wondering if he would get his family back. He did sigh in relief that Trisha didn't have sex with Ryan, while she was gone. "I understand, Trisha…" She nodded and then stood from the couch, as he looked up at her; he followed her lead and stood up as well. "I think we need a longer break, because it's not just your family, but it's your friends too. I don't want to make you choose either and I'm not. I think you are a great dad and…" Vance interjected. "Wait a minute, Trisha, don't do this…we're not the same people anymore; I changed and you did too. I've been giving you and the kids my all, since we got back together. I have another chance to do right by you and make this work, so let me."

Trisha turned her head to the side and then Vance sighed. "Baby, if you want space, then can you have your space here with the kids? I will leave and you can stay here, at home, with the kids; I just don't want you to leave me." Trisha looked back at him. "So, if me and the kids return, then you will leave?" Vance nodded. "Yes…but I'd like to still be able to come home and see the kids. I can watch them or they can stay with me on the weekends." Trisha sighed and then nodded. "Ok…" Vance nodded. "Ok, well, I'll go pack some things and then leave." Vance turned around and was about to walk out the living room, when Trisha stopped him; he looked back at her, as she spoke. "I love you…" Vance slightly smiled. "I love you too…" Vance turned back around and then walked to the bedroom; Trisha sighed and then went to leave, to go get the kids and their things.

Chapter 30

Jordan walked out the bedroom to hear noise; he rolled his eyes and then walked to the living room, to see Dimitri sitting on the floor, while leaned back against the couch, Ju also sitting on the floor and playing with Jaelyn, Joron sitting on the couch, and Vance sitting on the couch as well; Cinco was on the other armchair. The guys were talking, while the television was on. Jordan shook his head. "I don't know why I believe I'm going to walk out my bedroom to peace and quiet, every day." Dimitri shot him a look. "And I don't know why I believe that every time I stay over here, that I'm not going to be woken up in the early morning hours, by you." Jordan rolled his eyes, as the guys laughed.

Cinco stood from the armchair and then went over to Jordan; he kissed him, as Joron sucked his teeth and Dimitri frowned. Vance shook his head and then Dimitri interjected. "Jordan, there are kids in the room." The guys stopped and then looked at Dimitri; Jordan made a sarcastic sound. "Please, Ju already knows how his Uncle Jordan gets down." Vance and Joron laughed, as Dimitri rolled his eyes. Ju looked at Dimitri. "He's right, Uncle Dimitri…my math teacher from last year likes men, but nobody knows, not even the girl teachers. I saw him in the parking lot kissing another man, when I had detention." Dimitri frowned, as Vance shook his head.

Jordan slightly leaned his head to the side. "Is that right? You said your math teacher?" Cinco shot him a look. "I think you're a little bit too interested in whoever this dude is." Jordan put his hands up and then dropped it. "I need a drink…and after I get my drink, then you can tell me why you are here, Vance." Vance knew that Jordan was going to get to him. "I…well, me and Trisha talked; she came over and we talked. I don't have her back, all the way yet, but I told her if she returned home with the kids, then I would leave." Jordan slowly turned around at the bar and looked at Vance; he shook his head. "Do I look like the Holiday Inn? Why am I the "go to" guy for everyone to come stay with?" Dimitri made a sarcastic sound. "Because you're older than everyone…all of us." Joron laughed and Jordan gave him a snide look. "You are the oldest, Dimitri…" Dimitri frowned and then looked around at everyone, before looking back at Jordan. "Damn, you're right…never mind."

Vance rolled his eyes. Jordan shook his head, as he made his drink and then went to sit down; Cinco sat down in front of the armchair, Jordan was in. While the guys talked, the doorbell rang. Vance said he would get it, so he got up and then walked out the living room; shortly after, he returned with Jaeda behind him. Vance returned to his seat, as Jaeda stood there and looked around at everyone. "Uh, is this like a guy slumber party or something?" Jordan frowned, as Dimitri nodded. "Yep, with the exception of your daughter." Vance slightly laughed, as Ju got up from the floor and went over to his mama; she smiled, as she hugged him and then Joron picked up Jaelyn to take her over to Jaeda. Jaeda took Jaelyn from Joron and then he looked at her. "Make sure they back by six." Jaeda frowned, as everyone looked at Joron.

She sarcastically laughed. "Are you serious, Joron? I think you're going too far with all this; these are still my kids and we're not divorced." Joron sucked his teeth. "We can be…" Jaeda sighed and then nodded. "I'm not gonna argue with you, Joron…" Jaeda looked at Ju. "Go get you and Jaelyn's stuff." Joron frowned. "You not taking them, so you can turn around and leave without them, if you want." Jaeda shot back. "Since when are you Ju's daddy?" Joron clenched his jaw and then shot Ju a look. "Take your sister and y'all go to the room." Ju looked at his mama and then back to Joron; he took Jaelyn from her and then walked out the living room, as she watched them. "Ju…" She looked back at Joron, but he spoke before she did. "I became his damn daddy right after Rendell died. You wanted a man to accept your son, well I did, and now you complaining about that." Jaeda spoke. "I'm not complaining about anything…"

Both continued to argue, as Dimitri put his hand over his face; Vance frowned, several times and couldn't believe they were arguing in the first place. Jordan stood from the chair and tried to diffuse the situation, but failed. Joron threw his hands up. "Just get the fuck out and take your ass back to the barbecue man." Cinco frowned, as Jaeda stared at Joron and then shook her head. "Fine, I'll do that then…" She was about to leave, when he stopped her with his words. "Don't fucking play with me, Jaeda." She stopped and then looked back at him. "Excuse me?" Joron stared angrily at her. "Don't fucking play with me…don't try to take my kids from me, and after you drop the load, you carrying now, I'ma take that baby from you too." Jordan frowned, as he looked at his brother, while the guys were in disbelief of Joron's behavior.

Jaeda made a sarcastic sound. "I don't know what's wrong with you, Joron, but right now I don't care. I'ma go get my kids and get them away from you because you're losing your damn mind." Jaeda turned around to go get the kids and Joron became enraged; he rushed Jaeda before any of them could blink. Joron grabbed Jaeda and then slammed her against the wall. The guys jumped up and then ran over, as Joron had Jaeda pinned and had his arm to her throat. "You're not taking my kids!" Jordan and Cinco grabbed Joron. "Let her go, Ron!" They were able to pull Joron back from Jaeda and she started to cough hysterically, as Dimitri and Vance held her on both sides.

Jordan pushed Joron so hard, that he fell back into the living room. "What the fuck is your problem!" Joron looked at his brother and then pushed him out the way, to get to Jaeda. "Baby, let me talk to you…I'm sorry." Jaeda pushed Dimitri out her way to get behind him. Vance shook his head, no. "Ron, leave her alone!" Joron shook his head. "Jaeda, baby, I'm sorry…I'm not gonna hurt you; I wouldn't hurt you."

Jaeda looked at Jordan. "I want my kids." He nodded and Joron snapped again. "Didn't you fucking hear what I said! I'm not gonna hurt you and you're not taking my kids!" Dimitri threw his hands up. "For God's sake, Ron…calm the fuck down." Jordan interjected, as Cinco and Vance blocked Joron. "Jaeda, just go…I'll bring the kids to you later." Jaeda nodded and then turned around to leave; right after she left, the guys all looked at Joron. He looked around at them. "What?" Vance put his hand over his face and then walked around Joron, to go sit back down. Jordan stared at his brother while in disgust. "Ron, what the fuck is wrong with you? You slammed your pregnant wife against the damn wall and put your arm to her throat." Joron shook his head. "I didn't mean to do that, I just…I love my kids and she's trying to take them away from me; she's trying to get with that other nigga…and."

Jordan interjected. "Ron, slow down…you're not making any sense. I think you are losing your damn mind." Jordan walked around his brother and then went back to sit down, as Cinco sighed and then followed his lead. Joron rubbed his hands down his face and then walked out the living room, to go check on the kids.

Chapter 31

Trisha was back at the house with the kids; she was actually happy to be back at home and for the children to be back with their things. The kids were playing in the room, when the doorbell rang. Trisha went to the front and then opened the door to see Arianna. "Trisha…hey; uh, is Vance here?" Trisha shook her head. "No, it's just me and the kids." Arianna nodded. "Alright, well, are you two back together?" Trisha sighed. "No, we're not; he moved out for a while and me and the kids are back at home." Arianna slowly nodded her head and then asked to come in. Trisha was hesitant, but decided to let Arianna in, anyway; she stepped aside and Arianna walked in. After she closed the door, both women walked to the living room and then sat down on the couch.

Arianna slightly smiled, as Trisha stared at her. "So, Trisha…how is it going?" Trisha raised an eyebrow. "I left my husband, that is how it's going." Arianna wanted to speak to Vance, but decided since she got Trisha instead, that maybe she should try a different approach to this situation between Vance and Trisha. "Alright look, Trisha, I know what's going on between you and Vance…" Trisha interjected. "Big surprise, but I'm not interested in anything you have to say, Arianna; out of everyone, you were the worst to be around. You are such a bitch and coldhearted towards anyone that is not in your circle. I thought you were my friend, but I guess I was just naïve to think that you could be another woman's friend."

Arianna raised an eyebrow and then slightly laughed; she nodded her head. "That is good, Trisha…that was really good, but put a little more passion in that rant next time." Trisha frowned and then abruptly stood from the couch. "Are you mocking me, Arianna?" Arianna stood from the couch and then shook her head. "I'm not mocking you. I'm being very serious…you see, your problem is that you keep all your feelings and emotions, inside; you let other people walk all over you. You let Shavon take your husband…you let Vance talk to you and treat you like shit, and now here we all are again." Trisha was in disbelief and speechless; she didn't think her conversation with Arianna was going to go this way. Trisha turned her head to the side and then back to Arianna.

Arianna sat back down on the couch and then crossed her legs; she then lit a cigarette, as Trisha watched her. Afterwards, Arianna blew smoke out her mouth and nose. "Sit down, Trisha…" Trisha sighed and then sat back down on the couch; she also crossed her legs. Arianna slightly smiled. "I am a bitch…I enjoy being a bitch; that is my trademark, Trisha. You can't hurt my feelings and nothing you just said, has, but I wanted to let you know that we can be friends. And that, Vance loves you so much…we haven't seen him like this before, not even with Shavon. We all made mistakes in the past, but we learned from them and moved on. Vance fell in love with you again and he loves his children, so I'm asking you what will it take for you to take him back?"

Trisha sighed and then cleared her throat. "Can I have a cigarette?" Arianna slightly laughed and then nodded; she grabbed a cigarette and then handed one to her, along with a lighter. Trisha lit the cigarette and then took a puff; she closed her eyes and then opened them, as she blew smoke out her mouth. "I needed that…" Arianna nodded and Trisha sighed. "My biggest concern is that Vance could cheat on me again; that is my biggest fear and I don't know if I can take that again. We have kids now and I don't want our kids to go through a messy divorce or see their parents fighting." Arianna sighed. "I get that, Trisha, but Vance didn't cheat on you with multiple women…it was just one woman; and she is insignificant now…has been since before you and Vance got back together. We all have personally seen a big change in Vance, so this is it for him; he is serious about you and his kids…and being dedicated to only you."

Trisha shook her head. "How can I believe you, Arianna? You lied to me for so long when me and Vance were married the first time around." Arianna looked around and then put her cigarette out in the ashtray; she then got back to Trisha. "Because Vance is one of my good friends and I love him…we all love each other and we would do anything to make sure that we're all happy and safe. I'm aware that I was a big problem for you too, so I want to make it right on my end. I want you to be around us, but if you're going to do that, then you need to relax and loosen up; you can't take everything to heart and you have to learn how to have fun. I'm the only female in a big group of guys and I'm probably the worst talking one; you don't have to be like me, but you can at least try to fit yourself in somewhere. And maybe it's time you confront Shavon, not try to be her friend; Vance confronted her, but honestly, Trisha, that was your job. I would have been set any bitch straight for fucking with what was mine and I think you know that already. Show Vance that no one is going to walk all over you again."

Trisha sat there and stared at Arianna, as she spoke; she slightly frowned and felt she made valid points. Trisha slightly laughed, as Arianna handed her the ashtray; she put the cigarette out and then slightly laughed again. "I paid hundreds of dollars to my therapist and everything you just said was clearer than anything he ever said." Arianna smiled and then nodded; she then stood from the couch, as Trisha followed her lead. Arianna looked around and then back to Trisha. "I'm having a birthday party for Marc, at the office, after hours, this Friday. I want you to come and with a different attitude. I want you to walk up in that bitch like you know you are the shit, but not in a stuck-up way, like you use to." Trisha rolled her eyes at Arianna's last comment and then nodded.

Arianna grinned. "And everyone will be there, in the group, along with an extra guest, that I'm inviting just for you. The thing is, Trisha, some people you are better than…and Shavon is one of them. So, Friday night, get your kids situated, and wear your best, because we are going to have fun and you are going to show your ass." Trisha had her mouth slightly open, but nodded; she closed her mouth and then cleared her throat. Arianna smiled. "I won't tell anyone that you're coming, so you can make a big entrance." Trisha nodded and then Arianna put her hand out; Trisha took her hand and they shook on it. Afterwards, Arianna said she had to go and Trisha walked her out. After Arianna was gone, Trisha turned around at the front door and then sighed.

Chapter 32

It was Friday night and everyone was getting ready for Marc's thirty-third birthday party, at the office; Arianna was already there, as well as others. Marc walked over to her and she turned around; Arianna smiled, as he rolled his eyes. "You never cease to amaze me, Arianna. The fact that you're throwing me a birthday party, is suspect." Arianna frowned, as she stared at him. "We've been good for a while, Marc, so what are you suspecting now?" Marc sighed. "Blackmail is still hovering over my damn head every day." Arianna shook her head. "Really, Marc? They dropped the charges and Myra is out; there are no suspects and we're good, have been. I put that all behind me and you should too; Ethan is dead too." Marc put his hand up and then dropped it. "Fine, Arianna…I'll drop it, but I'm dating someone now. I don't know why, but I want you to meet her." Arianna nodded. "Ok, sounds good, Marc; well regardless, I want you to have a good time, because I damn sure am." Arianna walked away, as Marc frowned and wondered what she meant by that. He disregarded her comment and then went to get a drink; shortly after, many people were there already and enjoying themselves. Dimitri was in town and had Valerie with him; Valerie and Ashley had a cousin that lived in Fort Worth, so the kids were in Fort Worth with her. Both felt they could relax and drink as much as they wanted, while having a break from the kids.

Vance walked in along with Joron; Jordan and Cinco were right behind them. The guys got together and slapped hands, before they started to speak. The employees who worked there, were there as well, including Leslie; Arianna invited Amber too. Marc's new woman was there already and Marc went over to Arianna to introduce her, as she stood with Amber.

Jorvik had a drink and then walked over to the guys; Arianna was right behind him after speaking to Marc and his girlfriend. Dimitri smiled. "As usual, Arianna, you look good…" Valerie glanced at him, as Arianna smiled. "Thank you, Dimitri…all of you guys look good yourselves…" She looked at Jordan. "You are glowing, Jordan." Jordan rolled his eyes, as the guys laughed. Valerie sighed, as she stood there and felt as Trisha did: uncomfortable and that she didn't fit in. Valerie looked and then saw Jaeda walk in; she sighed in relief and then excused herself from Dimitri and the others.

After she walked away, Dimitri looked to where she was going. "Jaeda is here…" They all turned and then saw Jaeda and her belly, along with her outfit. Arianna slightly frowned. "What is she wearing?" Joron made a sarcastic sound. "Her work uniform…" The guys looked at Joron and then back to Jaeda. Arianna slightly laughed. "Wow…she is working that tank top." Jorvik frowned, as Jordan and the others laughed. Joron shook his head. "Thanks, Arianna…" She rolled her eyes and then lit a cigarette.

Valerie walked over to Jaeda and she looked at her. "Hey…" Jaeda nodded. "Uh, hey." Valerie sighed. "I know the last time we saw each other and talked, was bad, but I didn't think you were gonna stop talking to me for good." Jaeda sighed and then nodded. "Yeah well, if you were gonna keep talking the same way Shavon was, then I guess our friendship was gonna be over regardless." Valerie nodded and understood. "I thought about it and you were right…hell, Vance was right to go off the way he did. I thought we were all good and moved on, but Shavon didn't. I talked to her and she's still in love with Vance and wants him back."

Jaeda frowned and then shook her head. "What the…what happened to Randy?" Valerie made a sarcastic sound. "He overheard Shavon and Miss Brooks talking…and it's not what you think; he called his mama over to talk to Shavon, because she was depressed. Anyways, he heard their whole conversation and Shavon is stuck on Vance; she said it wasn't fair, and that she and Vance are supposed to be together. So, Randy broke up with her and apparently Vance told her, he wanted her out his life for good."

Jaeda was outdone and had missed so much, not talking to either woman, but didn't regret it. "Well, I hope Shavon gets herself together, but I'm not in that mess. I have my own problems and I can't focus on Shavon trying to move backwards, when everybody else is moving forward, and been moving forward." Valerie nodded. "Yeah, I love her, but she was talking a little bit too crazy for me." Jaeda shrugged her shoulders and then Valerie cleared her throat, as she looked at Jaeda's outfit. "Uh Jaeda, so what do you have going on...does it have something to do with that outfit?" Jaeda rolled her eyes and then laughed, as Valerie did too; Jaeda sighed and then explained, as Valerie listened.

Chapter 33

As the party continued, Leslie walked over to Jordan and Cinco; Jorvik slightly frowned, as Vance had flashbacks of the club fights. Leslie slightly smiled, as Cinco frowned. "What the hell you doing here?" Leslie looked from Jordan and then to Cinco. "I work here..." Cinco gave Leslie a snide look, as the guys sipped their drinks and looked on. Leslie grinned. "You got me the last time, since you had to use brass knuckles and couldn't fight without them." Jordan sighed, as Cinco slightly laughed. "Well, I'm left-handed...so I didn't wanna mess up my wedding band." Cinco lifted his hand up and grinned, as he showed his ring to Leslie. Joron slightly laughed, as he shook his head. Jorvik shook his head. "That sounds like, checkmate." Arianna looked at him and laughed to herself.

Leslie clenched his jaw and then nodded his head. "Yeah, whatever…" Leslie then looked at Jordan. "Can I talk to you, Jordan, in private?" Cinco interjected. "Hell no…why don't you get back with your ex-husband or have a damn threesome with him and my cousin; that fool is always clueless and confused, so he'd never suspect you want Terry back?" Jordan looked at Cinco and then slightly laughed, as Leslie had enough. "Why don't I have a threesome with you and Jordan?" Vance choked on his drink, as Joron's jaw dropped. Arianna cleared her throat and all were in suspense of what Jordan was going to say.

Jordan looked at Leslie and stared at him. Cinco looked at him and then did a doubletake; he frowned. "Jordan…" Leslie grinned and then slightly laughed, as he looked from Jordan and then back to Cinco. "It's on Jordan's mind now, so I think I got checkmate, bitch…" Leslie walked away from them and Jordan cleared his throat; Cinco continued to frown, as Jordan looked around at all of them. "It's hot in here…does anyone else need a cold drink?" Jordan walked away and Cinco threw his hands up. Dimitri and the others laughed, as Cinco found nothing funny. "Is that the damn trigger word for Jordan…threesome, and he forgets his damn senses?"

Vance put his hand up. "I plead the damn fifth…" Joron laughed, as Jorvik shook his head. "I think Jordan and Arianna have more exes running around, than any of us combined." Arianna frowned, as she looked at him. "Me and Marc are friends." Jorvik frowned. "I'm talking about Amber…that is you and Jordan's sexual conquest, right? She's over there…" They all turned and saw Amber. Arianna shook her head, no. "I had a threesome with her, but that is Jordan's bitch." Arianna realized what she said and put her hand over her face, as Dimitri and the guys laughed.

Cinco threw his hands up. "That's Amber?" Dimitri interjected. "Yes, but she is used a lot for her sexual services, from what I heard." Joron frowned, as Arianna and Jorvik laughed. Cinco rubbed his hands down his face and then sighed. Shortly after, Jordan returned with a drink.

Joron kept staring at Jaeda off and on, as she spoke and laughed with Valerie. Not too long after, Lillian and Lawrence walked in with Daniel; Joron frowned. "What the fuck?" The guys looked at him and then turned to where he was looking; they all saw Vance's mama, her husband, and another guy. Arianna spoke. "Who is the guy?" Jorvik cleared his throat. "That is Vance's step brother, Daniel." They all looked at him and then back to Joron, who then spoke. "I see everybody wanna fuck with me tonight." Arianna frowned, as Dimitri threw his hand up. "Please Ron, we don't have the energy, to break up any fights tonight. I didn't come in town for this." Jorvik laughed, as Vance shook his head.

Joron slowly nodded his head, as he continued to stare. "It's cool, I don't gonna say shit…or do nothing, unless he touch her." The guys frowned, as Arianna spoke. "Touch her? What is he going to do, finger her in front of everyone?" Jorvik put his hand over his face, as Vance frowned, and Jordan laughed. Joron shot her a look. "Shut up, Arianna…just like I said before, pregnancy pussy." Vance rolled his eyes and Jorvik shook his head, no. "Don't…I don't want to hear any more about pregnancy pussy, Ron." Dimitri laughed, as Arianna joined him; Jordan rolled his eyes. Joron sighed and then continued to stare.

Chapter 34

Lillian and Lawrence broke away from Daniel, who was with Jaeda and Valerie now, when Lillian saw Vance; they went over to Vance and the others. Lillian smiled. "Good to see you, Vance…and thanks for the invite, Arianna." They all looked at Arianna; she smiled and then nodded. "No problem, Mr. and Mrs. Henderson; we are all family in some form." Vance frowned, as Joron shot her a look. "Family, huh?" Joron looked at Lillian and Lawrence. "Why your son, fucking my wife?" Vance sighed, as Dimitri shook his head; Jordan sipped his drink. Lillian and Lawrence looked at each other and then back to Joron; Lawrence spoke. "What?" Joron nodded. "Why is your son, Daniel, fucking my pregnant wife?" Lawrence frowned and then looked at Lillian. "It's the pregnancy pussy I keep hearing about, right?" Arianna put her hand over her face and laughed hard, as Jorvik turned his head away to laugh. Lillian frowned and was disgusted, as she looked at her husband. "What?"

Lawrence put his hand up and then cleared his throat; he looked back at Joron. "Look, I don't know what you think, but Daniel wouldn't cheat with a married woman; from what I heard, he and Jaeda are just friends, and have been since they both lived in Atlanta." Lillian frowned. "I didn't know that." Vance made a sarcastic sound. "I thought you knew everything, mama." Lillian looked at him and rolled her eyes. "I can spot out sidelines, not random infidelity." Lawrence looked at her. "You can spot out, what?" Lillian cleared her throat and then shook her head. "Forget it...if Daniel was cheating with Jaeda, then I would know." She turned to look at them and then shook her head. "No, there is no sex between them...the body language is all wrong, and not common for infidelity. He is being a good friend...but I can sense that he does have a crush on her; regardless, he hasn't made a move." Joron frowned, as Vance raised an eyebrow; Dimitri and Arianna looked at each other, before Dimitri spoke. "It's really true about you...that is amazing; it's like you are an infidelity psychic." Arianna laughed, as Lawrence frowned and had no words to say to that.

Joron spoke. "Well, if he not doing nothing, then why he staring at her like that?" They all looked and then Lillian raised an eyebrow. "He is not staring at her...but at her stomach; maybe he has a little fetish...Lawrence." She looked at her husband and he looked back at her; he saw how she was staring at him and then threw his hands up. "Why are you looking at me like that? I don't even know what you're talking about." Lillian crossed her arms, as the guys were confused. "Lawrence, you know something, so either you say it or I will take another psychic guess." He sighed. "Ok, maybe Daniel does have a little pregnancy fetish…since high school; but he knows how to control it." Arianna slightly leaned her head to the side, as she stared at Daniel. "Yeah, he can control it alright…but his hard dick says otherwise." The guys shot her a look, especially Jorvik. "I think you are staring too hard if you can see that from here." She looked at him and frowned, as Jordan laughed. "Everyone has a gift, Vik, and unfortunately that is one of Arianna's." He laughed, as Dimitri and Vance did too.

Lawrence rolled his eyes and Lillian shook her head, as she turned around to everyone. "Well, it is still apparent that Daniel wouldn't cross that line, but he is very much enjoying himself while being in Jaeda's presence." Lawrence shot her a look; Joron frowned and then sucked his teeth. Dimitri put his hand up, before Joron exploded. "Ron, just let the man look…he is not hurting anyone; he is apparently not going to touch her, so what is the harm?" Arianna frowned, as Joron shot Dimitri a look.

Jordan raised an eyebrow and was now intrigued with the conversation. Lawrence cleared his throat, as Vance looked at Dimitri. "Would you want a man staring at Val like that, for sexual reasons?" Dimitri made a sarcastic sound. "Uh Vance, I took a few pages out of Jordan's book of erotica…and I can honestly say that it's a turn on, for me to watch a man stare at my wife, like he wants to fuck her; and we purposely went out together and acted as if we didn't know each other, just for that reason. Then we go home and fuck like jackrabbits." Joron couldn't help it and had to laugh, as Jorvik and Jordan did too. Dimitri and Jordan actually slapped hands on that one.

Lillian raised an eyebrow and Lawrence cleared his throat, while uncomfortable with the conversation. Arianna shook her head. "Wow, Dimitri…but Jordan still has you beat, since it is his erotica book, you took pages from. Instead of the regular fantasy of threesomes, Jordan is way past that and won't be satisfied until he can have a full-blown orgy with four plus people." Dimitri frowned, as Vance and the guys laughed. Jordan rolled his eyes. "Whatever, Arianna." Joron put his hands up. "Can we get back to me?" They all looked at him and Lillian sighed. "Joron, Jaeda is not cheating on you; but I'm sure you've already made it difficult for her anyway, because you thought she was. Do as Dimitri…enjoy another man wanting your woman, but can't have her." Lawrence frowned, as well as Vance. "Mama, I don't want to hear any sexual advice come out your mouth. I don't even want to talk about it." Lillian raised an eyebrow and then sarcastically laughed. "Uh Dimitri, did you enjoy the thing Valerie did with her tongue and the fruit?" Dimitri's jaw dropped, as he looked at Lillian; Arianna raised an eyebrow and looked between them.

Dimitri started to stutter, as he spoke. "Why?" Lillian grinned and Lawrence cleared his throat. "Uh Dimitri, I already know what she's talking about, so just say, yes." Lawrence grinned at Lillian, while Vance was disgusted. "Oh my God…" Dimitri shook his head. "I had no idea…that was your advice?" Jorvik frowned and wanted the conversation changed, as they knew

Vance did. "Mama, please stop…you made your point…and later on, me and Dimitri can talk, so I find out exactly what that fruit thing is." Jordan and Arianna laughed, as Joron shook his head.

Before another word could be said, they all heard yelling and turned around. Jorvik sighed. "Jordan, that's you…" Jordan looked at his brother and then rolled his eyes.

Chapter 35

Cinco had already ducked away from the group after Jordan returned; he went to get a drink at a table and had to clear his mind. Leslie walked over and Cinco turned his head to him; he rolled his eyes and then sighed, as he went back to making his drink. "What you want, Leslie?" Leslie looked around and then back to Cinco. "I was curious about what Jordan said, after I left y'all." Cinco clenched his jaw and then shook his head. "Why don't you just leave us alone? He don't want you…how many times he gotta tell you that?" Cinco turned all the way around to Leslie this time. Leslie slightly grinned. "For one, he never said that he don't want me…regardless, Jordan will always want me, Cinco…I know that's hard for you to hear, but it's true. I know what Jordan likes and how he likes it; he can't help himself and when the opportunity presents itself, he gets an urge to go for it. Ever since he caught us…seeing us together the way we were, I know he automatically thought about the three of us being together…or maybe he just thought about me and him being together."

Cinco turned his head to the side and then back to Leslie. "Never gonna happen…you were stupid enough to share, but I'm not. I got the fucking ring…something you don't got with Jordan; something no guy ever got with him before, not even Tyler. All y'all exes want what I got, but y'all are never gonna get it, and you can't fucking stand it, can you Les?" Cinco stepped closer to Leslie and got in his face. "It kills you that Jordan moved on with me, don't it? That after a few months, I stepped right in his life and got him, when you were trying for so long and got dismissed." Leslie clenched his jaw. "Get out my face, Cinco." Cinco grinned and then shook his head, no. "What's the matter, Les…you starting to realize that I'm right and you never gonna be back in Jordan's bed again? It's true, because your dick is something, he's never gonna see again." Leslie had enough and pushed Cinco out his face; he then punched him in the face. "You fucking bitch!"

Cinco fell back into the table and Leslie went back in to punch him again. Both guys were fighting and then Jordan and others ran over. Leslie punched Cinco again and then pushed him back; he saw Jordan come over to him and then looked at Cinco. "He won't see this dick again, huh!" Leslie turned to Jordan and then quickly unzipped his jeans; he then pulled his dick out and stroked it, so it could get hard. Afterwards, he stepped back and put his arms out.

Jaws dropped, as the cigarette fell out of Marc's mouth, when he saw the display. "Come on, Jordan! You can't tell me you don't want this anymore!" Jordan stopped in his tracks and stared hard, as Leslie smiled. Cinco shot Jordan a look. "What the fuck, Jordan!" Arianna went over and Jorvik frowned, as he went after her. Arianna grabbed Jordan and turned him around. "Get a grip, Jordan…" Leslie smiled and then put this dick back in; he then zipped up, as he looked at Cinco. "He won't see what again, Cinco? Fuck you." Leslie said nothing else and then turned around to leave the office, while people were left stunned and disgusted at the same time.

Arianna pushed Jordan to a chair and then sat him down; Jorvik went over, as well as the others. "What the hell?" Arianna laughed, while none of the guys found anything funny. Jordan looked at Arianna. "I'm fine, Arianna." He stood from the chair and then waved his hand around, while Dimitri put his hand over his face. Vance shook his head. "I don't know what you do to the people you fuck, but you turn all of them into lunatics after you dump them." Dimitri and Joron laughed, as Arianna shook her head. "That was one hell of a show." Jorvik shot her a look. "I bet it was, since you were one of the first to go over and investigate." She gave him a snide look and Jordan rolled his eyes. "I expect this from Tyler, if he was still alive, not Les; Amber doesn't even act like this."

Cinco walked over and Jordan sighed; he shook his head. "Look Cinco…I." Cinco interjected, as he put his hand up. "Don't, Jordan…I don't even know what to say, except this shit is my fault. I brought that dude back in your life, because I was stupid. Now he won't go away and I'm tired of fighting him…" Jordan frowned. "So, what the hell are you saying, Cinco?" Cinco shrugged his shoulders. "I don't know, I'm just tired…I'm going home." Cinco turned around and then walked away to leave. Jordan threw his hands up and then shook his head. As Cinco was walking out, he passed by someone; it was Shavon.

Chapter 36

Shavon walked in, while unaware of what transpired already. Lillian turned her head and then raised an eyebrow, while unaware that Shavon was going to be there. She looked at Vance, but he was distracted, so didn't see Shavon walk in. Valerie and Jaeda turned their heads and Valerie sighed. "I wonder what's about to happen now?" Jaeda shook her head, as Daniel stood next to her. "That's Randy's woman, right?" Jaeda looked at him. "Uh, no…Randy broke up with her, because she's still in love with Vance." Daniel frowned. "Vance? Randy's brother, Vance? My stepbrother, Vance?" The women looked at him and slowly nodded their heads. Jaeda made a sarcastic sound. "There's a lot you don't know and too little time to explain it to you now." Daniel rolled his eyes and then they all turned their heads, to see Shavon walk over to Vance.

Vance turned around and saw Shavon; he frowned. "What are you doing here?" Shavon looked around at everyone and then back to him. "You invited me." Vance frowned and then shook his head. "No, I didn't." Arianna interjected. "Uh hey, Shavon…Vance didn't invite you…I did." Vance frowned, as he and everyone looked at Arianna. "Arianna, what the hell are you doing?" Shavon frowned. "What you invite me for?" Arianna looked at her watch and then around Shavon; she smiled, before looking back at Shavon. "Someone wanted to talk to you…uh, her."

Everyone turned around and saw Trisha walking towards them. Jorvik raised an eyebrow, as Lillian and Lawrence looked at each other. Jordan shook his head, as he eyed her. Shavon looked back at Arianna. "I don't wanna talk to her. I didn't come for her." Trisha made it over to everyone. "Well, who did you come here for?" Shavon turned around to Trisha and looked her up and down.

Vance shook his head; he grabbed Arianna and then whispered. "What the hell did you do?" Arianna shot him a look, and whispered back. "Do you want you your wife back or not?" Vance stared at her and then nodded; Arianna snatched her arm from him and then turned back to the women. Shavon cleared her throat. "Hey, Trisha…" Trisha stared at Shavon and then grinned. "I think you greeted me wrong…you should have said, hey, Mrs. Brooks…Mrs. Vance Brooks, because that is who the fuck I am. I'm Vance's wife now just like I was before. I should have done this a long time ago, but I needed a little push, so I'm doing it now." Vance raised an eyebrow and then looked at Arianna, while Dimitri said nothing and wanted to see where this was going.

Shavon slightly laughed and then shook her head. "You needed a push, huh? Why you need a push now? You worried that your husband might want me back?" Joron looked at the others and then back to the women. Trisha smiled. "Actually Shavon, I'm not worried about a damn thing and even though I appreciate my husband standing up for me, I need to do this myself. You are not a threat to me and I know Vance doesn't want you back…Randy doesn't even want you back." Shavon clenched her jaw, as she stared at Trisha. "Yeah, it's cool…Trisha, it must make you feel good to have Vance sister's leftovers."

Vance's jaw dropped and Dimitri put his hand over his face. Lillian shot her son a look and Lawrence frowned. Trisha laughed and then shook her head. "I didn't have anyone's leftovers…everyone after me had my damn leftovers, and that includes you. And in case you forgot, Lily is dead; I shot that bitch and don't think I won't do the same to you, if you keep parading around my husband like he is yours. Everyone knows you're still in love with him and want him back, but it's too late, sweetie…I'm the head bitch again." Shavon became angry and then pushed Trisha out her face; Vance was about to react, but Arianna stopped him.

Trisha lunged at Shavon and then punched her in the face. Arianna smiled, as Trisha grabbed Shavon's face and then slammed it into the pillar, in the office. Trisha then kneed Shavon in the face, before she flung her to the floor. Trisha then took her heels off and Arianna laughed. "She's taking the heels off, gentlemen." Joron laughed; Jorvik shot her a look and Jordan frowned.

Shavon got up from the floor and Trisha signaled to Shavon, to bring it. Jaeda and Valerie looked at each other, before looking back at the women. "Come on, Shavon…I've been waiting for this, for years." Shavon grit her teeth, as they stared at each other. "You think you doing something, by getting a fucking backbone." Trisha moved around, as Shavon did the same. "I think about time you leave here, you're going to be crawling, not walking." Shavon had enough and then both women lunged at each other; Shavon slammed Trisha back against the pillar and then Trisha pushed Shavon back, before she elbowed her in the face. Shavon yelled and then Arianna ran past the women, as the guys watched. Arianna grabbed something from the table, as Valerie and Jaeda watched her. Arianna yelled. "Trisha!" Arianna tossed the bottle and Trisha caught it; before Shavon could lunge at Trisha again, Trisha swung the bottle and hit Shavon in the face, hard. The bottle broke and Shavon went down; she was out cold.

Lillian had her hand over her mouth, as Trisha dropped the broken bottle on the floor and then backed up, as the guys watched; she was breathing hard. Vance had his mouth open. "I don't think I've ever been this turned on in my life…that shit was so hot and my dick is hard." Dimitri frowned, as Joron shot him a look. "Nigga, get the hell away from me talking like that." Jordan laughed, as Lawrence did too.

Trisha went to Vance, as the guys moved out the way; she smiled. "I love you and I want you to come home…I don't care about Shavon or what anyone thinks about me. Arianna made me realize that I'm wasting time thinking about the past, when I have you again, right now. And just to make some things clear, right now, I don't want that bitch around me or you ever again; and I hope I've made myself clear enough." Vance started to stutter and then closed his mouth; he nodded his head, like a child. Trisha smiled and then nodded. "I need a damn drink…" Trisha turned around and walked away from him, as he stood there while speechless.

Arianna walked over to Vance and the guys; they looked at her. Dimitri shook his head. "Well, Vik, I think your wife deserves that standing ovation, now." Jordan laughed, as Jorvik gave Dimitri a snide look. Vance looked at her. "What the hell just happened? What did you tell her?" Arianna sighed. "Vance, I thought about what you said and you were right; Trisha is your wife again and we should all respect that, more so me. I had a little chat with Trisha and set this meeting up between her and Shavon, so Trisha could release all her anger on her, instead of you. You're welcome, Vance." Jordan rolled his eyes and Vance shook his head, as he hugged Arianna. "God bless you, Arianna." Jorvik frowned, as the guys laughed.

Shavon woke up and was helped up by other workers at the magazine. Marc, Jaeda, Daniel, and Valerie walked over. Marc shook his head, as he looked at Arianna. "Nice throw, Arianna." Arianna looked at Marc and then rolled her eyes. "Shut up, Marc, and happy birthday again." He frowned, as Jorvik rolled his eyes. Dimitri put his arm around Valerie from behind and held her, as Joron looked at Daniel; Jaeda looked at Joron. "Hey, Joron." The guys looked at Jaeda and then to Joron, who acted as if he didn't hear her.

Chapter 37

Jaeda sighed and then cleared her throat; she was about to walk away, when Joron turned his head and stopped her. "So, you and that nigga not fucking?" Daniel frowned, as Jordan threw his hands up. Lawrence looked at Lillian and then to his son. Jaeda crossed her arms. "No…" Daniel interjected. "What's with you, man? Your wife can't have friends?" Everyone looked at Daniel and then back to Joron. "Not a friend like you…I know what you want?" Lawrence put his hand over his face, while Dimitri shook his head. Daniel slightly nodded his head and then cleared his throat after he thought about it. "You think I want her, because she's pregnant, right?" Joron stared at him and Daniel felt he received his answer. Daniel shook his head. "No, that's not it…I already had Jaeda in Atlanta, so that's why I want her again."

Jorvik's jaw dropped, as Jaeda put her hand over her face. Joron became enraged and then pushed Lawrence out the way; he tackled Daniel and both went down to the floor.

Jaeda moved out the way, as the guys threw punches; Trisha walked over and Vance grabbed her hand to pull her to him. Jordan and Lawrence tried to pull the guys apart, but failed. Jaeda moved back and then put her hand to her stomach; she started to wince in pain. "Joron…" She wasn't loud enough with all the commotion and Valerie turned her head to Jaeda; she then looked back at the guys and yelled. "Joron!" The guys stopped and Jaeda almost fell back; Dimitri went over to Jaeda and held her up. "Ron, the baby is coming!" Joron and Daniel stopped; he pushed Daniel out his face and then ran over to Jaeda. "Baby, you alright?" Jaeda shook her head, no. Valerie interjected. "She's in labor, Joron, she needs to go to the damn hospital." Joron nodded and then he and Dimitri helped Jaeda walk, as she yelled out in pain; she yelled again and then shook her head. "Stop! I can't, the baby's coming now!"

The guys were in a panic, as Lillian went over and then told the guys to lay her down. Lillian went down and then looked around. "Someone bring me a blanket, and gloves." Amber went to retrieve the items, as everyone stood by. Joron got behind Jaeda and she laid against him. Amber quickly brought the blanket and gloves over to Lillian; Lillian put the gloves on, while Vance called an ambulance. Lillian covered Jaeda's lower half and then removed her clothes with her hands under the blanket. Jaeda yelled, as Joron held her against him. "It's alright, baby; I'm right here." Lillian looked at Jaeda. "I need you to push on the next contraction, Jaeda." Jaeda yelled in pain, as everyone cringed. Jaeda then pushed, as Joron had a good grip on her. Lillian nodded, with her hands under the blanket. "That's right, Jaeda…push again, even harder." Jaeda pushed hard, with her eyes closed and then opened them, after yelling in agonizing pain. Lillian smiled and then everyone heard the baby crying.

Jaeda put her head back against Joron, as he tried to see the baby; Amber gave Lillian another blanket, to wrap the baby in and then Lillian held the baby up, with a smile on her face. "It is a boy." Joron smiled. "Ah hell, yeah!" Jordan looked at his bother and laughed, as the others followed his lead. The door opened and the paramedics came in with the gurney and equipment.

As the paramedics were on the way to her, Jaeda started to convulse and everyone frowned. Joron held his wife, as she had a seizure. Joron was in a panic. "What's wrong with her!" The paramedics went over and then took over. One took the baby and then cut the umbilical cord, as the other put an oxygen mask over Jaeda's face. Lillian got out the way, and Joron had to be dragged away, so the paramedics could do their job. The paramedic handed Joron his son and then they put Jaeda on the gurney. After she was strapped in, Joron was told to follow them with the baby. Joron was confused, as he looked at his brothers, but did as he was told.

Jorvik told Arianna that they were going to the hospital and others decided to do the same. It wasn't too long after, that everyone was making their way out the office and to their cars, to head to the hospital.

Chapter 38

Once at the hospital, many were there and seated in the emergency room; Jorvik and Arianna, Trisha and Vance, Jordan, Dimitri and Valerie, Lillian and Lawrence, and Daniel. Joron was there, but wasn't around; everyone assumed he was with Jaeda and the baby.

As they all sat there and waited to hear anything, Joron walked from behind doors and then over to everyone. They all looked at him and Jordan stood from the chair, along with Jorvik. Joron looked at Jordan. "I need to talk to you and Vik." Jordan frowned and then Jorvik nodded; the guys walked away from everyone and once far enough away, they stopped. Jordan was concerned about his brother. "Ron, what's wrong? How is Jaeda?" Joron looked between his brothers. "The baby good, but they said Jaeda lost a lot of blood; she got preeclampsia or something." Jorvik nodded and then looked at Jordan; Jordan sighed. "We're sorry, Ron." Joron nodded and then cleared his throat. "Look, I gotta tell y'all something…but y'all can't tell Jaeda." The guys frowned and looked at each other again, before looking back at Joron.

Jorvik sighed. "Tell us, what?" Joron sucked his teeth. "I'm bi-polar…" Jordan frowned, while Jorvik was taken aback. "Seriously, Ron?" Joron nodded his head; he looked around and then back to his brothers again. "Yeah, I been bi-polar for a while and I take medication, but I stopped after I got with Jaeda; it got a few side effects that I don't like." Jordan was outdone. "You stopped taking medication for bi-polar disorder, because of side effects? Are you crazy, Ron? You can't just decide something like that on your own; and it makes sense now that you said it." Jorvik nodded his head and had to agree. Joron shook his head. "Look I know, but I didn't want Jaeda to catch me taking nothing, so I just stopped."

Jordan put his hand over his face and then dropped it. "Ron, you slammed Jaeda against the wall, so that wasn't a sign to you, that maybe you needed to start taking your meds again? Your whole relationship with Jaeda has been psychotic on your end; we know why now, but all the trouble you caused could have been prevented." Joron nodded and slightly looked down, before looking back up again at his brother. "Yeah, I know, but just don't tell her." Jorvik raised an eyebrow. "Ron…listen to me; there is nothing to be ashamed about being bi-polar and Jaeda is your wife that just had your second child. You can't hide this from her, because we are telling you, right now, to get back on your medication, before something happens that you can't take back…besides everything that already happened."

Joron sucked his teeth and then rubbed his hands down his face; he sighed and then nodded. Jordan and Jorvik were happy that they were able to talk some sense into their baby brother. Jordan hit Joron on the back and before another word, could be said, a doctor came out and Joron turned around; he went over to the doctor, as the guys followed him. Once at the doctor, Joron asked about his wife. The doctor smiled. "Jaeda is just fine now…we stopped the bleeding and she hasn't had another seizure; her blood pressure is normal now as well. And your son is doing just fine." Joron slightly smiled and then nodded, as Jordan and Jorvik smiled at him. Joron thanked the doctor and then was told he could see his wife.

Joron sighed with relief, as he swallowed hard; he looked at his brothers. "I'ma go see Jaeda, but can one of y'all call Dell and tell him what's going on? He got Ju and Jaelyn with him." Jordan nodded and said he would do it; Joron thanked his brother and then they hugged. Afterwards, Jordan said they all were going to leave and would return to see the baby, tomorrow. Joron nodded and then the guys walked back over to everyone; Joron left to go see Jaeda.

Shortly after, Joron walked in the room and saw Jaeda in the bed, while sitting up and holding their son. Jaeda looked up at him and then back to the baby, as he walked over to the bed. Joron stood by the bed and then sighed. "Can I hold him?" Jaeda looked at him and then nodded; she handed the baby to him and he carefully took his son. Joron smiled, as he looked down at him. "This is it, right?" He looked at her and she nodded her head; he slightly laughed and nodded too. "So, did you name him?" Jaeda sighed. "Yeah…Joel." Joron looked at him and then nodded. "Joel Ford…sounds good." Jaeda looked around and then he looked back at her. "I'm sorry…I been a damn ass to you, but I'm sorry for putting my hands on you. I swear I'ma never gonna do that again, I just lost it. I thought you were trying to take my kids away from me and I…" Joron stopped, as she looked at him.

Joron sucked his teeth and then handed Joel back to Jaeda; she took the baby and then looked back at Joron, as he spoke. "I…I'm bi-polar…" Jaeda frowned, as she stared at him. "What?" Joron looked down, as if he was embarrassed and then spoke again, as he looked back at her. "I'm bi-polar…I was taking medication when I met you, but I stopped; I didn't get permission or nothing, I just stopped on my own." Jaeda shook her head. "Why didn't you tell me? How could you just stop taking meds for that without consulting a doctor?" Joron pulled the chair over to her bed and then sat down on it. He shrugged his shoulders like a kid. "I don't know…I just didn't want you to look at me different, like I was crazy or something." Jaeda shook her head. "That's stupid, Ron…and I been looking at you like you're crazy, since I met you." Joron slightly laughed and she did too.

Joron nodded his head and then leaned in closer to her. "I love you and I'm sorry…but I wanna talk to you about what I said…about the, being a man, thing."

Jaeda interjected. "Joron, don't...I was thinking about what you said and you were right. I guess I just got a fear of being broke or something. I mean, Devonte and Rick, both wanted me dead for insurance money...I don't even wanna be close to that situation again, to give you a chance to bump me off." Joron frowned. "That's your reason? I thought...never mind, but uh baby, I wouldn't do no shit like that to you. I'm bipolar, not a sociopath..." She laughed and he did too; he stopped and then shook his head. "I'm not gonna bump you off, but I do want you to let me be your husband and take of you and the family. If you wanna work, then cool, but not hard that it's breaking your back. I don't cut for babysitters and nannies and shit like that, so if we can work around that, then I'm cool. I just want my wife and kids back, and I don't give a fuck about nothing else."

Jaeda nodded. "Alright, I'll stop working at Daniel's place and just be home for a while until Jaelyn and Joel get a little older. Ju will be older too and could help out." Joron nodded and then slightly smiled; his smile then faded when he thought about something. "Daniel...so y'all fucked in Atlanta?" Jaeda sighed and then nodded. "It was after I went back to Devonte and found out he was cheating on me with Corrina; it happened twice, but it never happened since he's been around this time." Joron nodded. "Yeah, alright...well, it don't matter no more, you're not gonna work at his spot, so that's done." Jaeda rolled her eyes and then nodded. She sighed. "And you're going back on your medication, right?" Joron nodded his head. "Yeah..." She nodded and then leaned over to give him a kiss; he smiled, after she pulled back from him. "I love you..."

He nodded. "I love you too…" Afterwards, they got back to the baby and smiled at him.

Chapter 39

Trisha and Vance had arrived back at their home, together; Trisha relieved the nanny, after checking on the twins. Afterwards, Trisha walked to the bedroom and Vance was right behind her; both didn't say much on the way home, but Vance didn't know what to say. Trisha sat down on the bed and was about to take her heels off, when Vance went over to her and then knelt down, to do it for her; she slightly laughed. "That is a first…" Vance took her heels off and then got up from the floor to sit down on the bed, next to her. He took her hand and then slightly laughed. "I just don't want to piss you off and get hit with a bottle." Trisha rolled her eyes and he laughed; she put her hand up and then dropped it. "Maybe I was a little aggressive tonight, but…" Vance interjected. "No, baby, it was…it was something, but it was supposed to happen. I can't say enough how sorry I am for making you feel uncomfortable and insignificant; that won't happen again and I meant everything I said about focusing on you and the kids."

Trisha slightly smiled and then nodded. "That's good to hear…I love you, Vance, and I meant what I said too. I don't want to see Shavon around you or us, again." Vance nodded. "She is gone, for good, baby…and if she does come back around, then I'm sure your sidekick, Arianna, will be more than happy to help you get rid of her." Trisha laughed and Vance did too; he stopped and then licked his lips, as he stared at her. "You know, watching you handle Shavon tonight…it did something to me, below the belt; it made me want to bend you over the drink table." Trisha grinned and then shook her head. "Wow, Vance; me beating up another woman, is a turn on, now?" Vance nodded his head. "I didn't know it was, until tonight, but hell yes…" Trisha stared at him and then grinned; she leaned in and then they kissed.

Trisha then pulled back from Vance and stood from the bed, as he watched her. Trisha removed her blouse and then let it fall to the floor; she then pulled her skirt down and he grinned, as he watched her remove her thong. Trisha was standing there naked and then walked over to the dresser; she bent over it and then turned her head back to Vance. "It's not a drink table, but I hope this will do." Vance stood from the bed and then made a sarcastic sound. "Yes, it'll do…I think we're going to make another set of twins tonight." Vance walked over to Trisha, as she slightly laughed; he unzipped his jeans, as she bit her bottom lip and waited for her husband to enter her from behind.

*   *   *

Jordan arrived home and was tired; he hung his keys on the wall and then walked to the bedroom; it was quiet in the house and he knew that everyone that was staying with him, was back at home with their spouses. Jordan walked in the bedroom and then saw Cinco sitting on the side of the bed; he closed the door behind him and Cinco turned his head to him. "It's late…" Jordan nodded, as he sat down on the couch and then started to take his shoes off. "Yes, it is…" Cinco slightly nodded his head. "Where you been?" Jordan looked up at Cinco from the couch. "You missed a lot after you left…Jaeda had her baby at the party and then started to have a seizure; we've all been at the hospital." Cinco frowned. "Is she alright?" Jordan nodded his head, as he stood from the couch. "Her and the baby are fine…she had a boy; I'm going to the hospital to see them tomorrow."

Cinco nodded and Jordan was about to go to the bathroom, to take a shower, when Cinco stood from the bed. "You talk to Les?" Jordan frowned, as he turned around to Cinco. "Look Cinco, I don't want to talk about Les." Cinco spoke. "But I do…" Jordan sighed and then nodded; he walked over to the couch and then sat back down, as Cinco stayed standing. "I been thinking since I got home and I uh, well if you want a threesome with Les, then we can do it." Jordan stared at Cinco, as if he was crazy and was also in disbelief. "Cinco, what the hell? I didn't say anything about a damn threesome with Les…he said that, not me." Cinco nodded. "I saw how you looked at him, Jordan…after he offered that and after he pulled his damn dick out for you." Jordan rolled his eyes and then slightly laughed. "I'm sorry, Cinco, it's not like I haven't seen it before…hell, you saw it too; you've fucked it too."

Jordan continued to laugh, while Cinco found nothing funny. "This shit not funny." Jordan stood from the couch. "Yes, it is…it is also stupid; look, Cinco…the three-way relationship between me, Les, and Amber disbanded, because they were too attached and started having feelings for me. I think the last thing you want is for Les to get attached to me again; you see how he's acting now." Jordan walked away and then to the bathroom, as Cinco followed him.

Once in the bathroom, Jordan turned the shower on and then started to remove his clothes, as Cinco spoke. "I just wanna make you happy and maybe a threesome with Les, will calm him down and satisfy you." Jordan turned around to Cinco and then sighed. "I'm good, Cinco, unless you are offering this, because you want to fuck him again. I already had Les, so I know how he is in the bedroom already; that was your first time with him." Cinco sucked his teeth and then shook his head. "That's not it, Jordan." Jordan had enough. "Then what is it!" Cinco stared at him, as Jordan continued. "What the fuck is it! We're back together now, so what the fuck is the problem? If I wanted Les again, then I could have been had him; in case you didn't realize, I don't have to ask for a damn thing…dick and pussy is thrown at me." Cinco sighed, as he turned his head to the side; Jordan rubbed his hands down his face and then dropped them, as he calmed himself down. "If you want to end this marriage and go back to just fucking, then fine…but I'm telling you this now, once you walk out the door, Les will replace you and I guarantee that he is going to fight harder to keep me, than you did."

Jordan turned around to get in the shower, as Cinco turned his head back to him. Cinco then turned around and walked out the bathroom; he went to sit down on the bed and then rubbed his hands down his face, while thinking about what to do. He was mentally and physically drained; mentally drained from the head games that Leslie was playing with him and physically drained from all the fighting with Leslie, he was doing.

Cinco heard the shower turn off and then turned his head; Jordan walked out a few moments later, while naked. He went to the dresser to get some underwear and then after he put them on, he walked over to the bed, as Cinco watched him. "Jordan…" Jordan got in the bed, as he spoke. "What?" Cinco sighed. "I love you." Cinco got under the covers, and then turned the light off; he got on his side, as Jordan sighed and then laid down to go to sleep.

Chapter 40

It was the next day; Vance went to the door, when the doorbell rang. He opened the door and saw Jordan; the guys slapped hands and then Dimitri was behind him. Arianna and Jorvik, were right behind, with Evan. Vance frowned. "Did all of you carpool over here?" Jorvik rolled his eyes, as Vance closed the door behind everyone; they all walked to the living room. Everyone started to sit down, everywhere. Jordan put his feet up on the coffee table. "I was tired of seeing all of you at my house, so I told everyone we were coming over here." Arianna laughed, as Vance gave Jordan a snide look. "Whatever, Jordan…drink, right?" He nodded and then Vance went to the bar. Arianna put Evan down, so he could walk and play. Vance spoke while at the bar. "Where is Val and Ron?" Dimitri spoke. "Val went to the hospital to see Jaeda and the baby." Jordan spoke. "Ron is there too…he took Dell and the kids." Vance nodded and then turned around to take the drink to Jordan.

Vance then sat down, as Arianna spoke. "Where is Trisha?" Vance grinned. "She is asleep…I told all of you it was a turn on for me, to watch her beat Shavon's ass." Jordan laughed, as Jorvik frowned. Dimitri laughed, as he shook his head. Arianna rolled her eyes. "Wow…" Arianna looked at Jordan. "You look well rested, Jordan." Jordan looked at her and frowned. "I don't see how…Cinco had words for me when I got home last night; he went on and on about making me happy and having a threesome with Les." Dimitri frowned, as Vance shook his head.

Jorvik shook his head as well. "You're married now and your relationship is still unstable." Arianna laughed and had to agree. "So, what did you say?" They all looked at Jordan; he looked around at everyone and frowned. "I told him, no…I didn't get married this time around to have threesomes and cheat; I'm trying to do right, but Cinco is making it hard." Arianna interjected. "Hard, like Les's dick last night?" Jorvik shot her a look and Dimitri was disgusted; Jordan laughed, as Vance did too. "I told you, Jordan, you turn your exes into lunatics after you dump them."

Jorvik sighed and then spoke. "Just have the damn threesome and calm Cinco down, if that's what it's going to take." Jordan looked at him. "Are you serious? You must not know about me and Les in the bedroom." Jorvik put his hand up. "And I don't want to know; I was just saying." Vance laughed and Arianna spoke. "No, Jordan has a point; I heard a lot from

Amber…Cinco fucked Les with just the two of them, but throw Jordan into the mix and Cinco is going to put his own self to shame." Dimitri put his head down and laughed, as the guys did too.

Jordan put his hand up. "Come on now, Arianna, that is my husband you're talking about. Besides, the way Les has been acting lately and the dirty tricks he's been pulling, I don't want him involved in any way with me and Cinco." Arianna nodded. "Ok, well Cinco was right about one thing, he did start this; if he would have never hired Les at the club, then none of this would be happening now. If Les was still married to Terry, then you could inform him of what his spouse was doing." Jordan waved his hand around. "But they're not married and Terry couldn't control Les, even when they were. I've been trying to think about what to do, but I can't come up with anything reasonable; one option, is to get back into another three-way relationship with both of them, but…" Dimitri interjected. "Wait a minute, what? How the hell are you going to do that, when you're married?" Jordan sighed and then shook his head. "Stay married to Cinco and invite Les into the relationship with us."

They all frowned, as they stared at Jordan and Vance spoke. "That is insane, even for you." Jordan threw his hand up and Arianna slightly leaned her head to the side. "You know, as retarded as that sounds…for Jordan, that could work. I mean, I get it…you are married now, Jordan, so if you invite Les in the relationship, then he will agree to anything, just to have you back again. You and Cinco can…" Jorvik interjected. "Are you drunk?" Arianna gave him a snide look and Dimitri interjected. "It sounds like you've been thinking about doing something like this too…maybe with you, Vik, and Marc." Vance and Jordan laughed, as Jorvik shot Dimitri a look; he made a sarcastic sound. "You must be drunk too…that shit would never happen." Arianna rolled her eyes and Jordan shook his head. "I think I know what to do…I need to talk to both of them, together. I'll talk to all of you later." They nodded to him, as he swallowed down the remainder of his drink; he set the glass down on the coffee table and then stood from the couch. They told him, goodbye, on the way out and then everyone got back to talking and hanging out.

Chapter 41

Jordan returned home and made a phone call on his way; he walked in the house and called out for Cinco. Cinco walked from down the hall and then saw Jordan coming his way. "Follow me to the living room." Cinco followed Jordan and once in the living room, Jordan told Cinco to sit down; he then went to the bar to make a drink. Cinco wasn't sure what this was about, but heard the urgency in Jordan's voice. "Uh, what's going on, Jordan?" The doorbell rang, as Jordan turned around from the bar. "Right on time…I'll be back." Jordan walked out the living room, as Cinco watched him; he then sighed.

Shortly after, Jordan walked back in the living room, with Leslie behind him. Leslie stopped when he saw Cinco and Cinco did a doubletake, when he saw

Leslie. Cinco looked at Jordan. "Why's he here?" Jordan looked at Cinco and then to Leslie. "Sit down, Les." Leslie sighed and then did as he was told. Jordan went back to the bar to get his drink and then went to sit down on the couch, as both guys stared at him.

Jordan sighed, as he looked between them; he set his glass down on the end table, after he took a sip and then lit a cigarette, as he spoke. "Alright, so tell me what you two want?" Cinco frowned, as Leslie raised an eyebrow. Leslie was confused. "Is that a trick question or something?" Jordan looked at him and then shook his head. "No, it's not…and I'm not playing; I'm very serious. Both of you are driving me crazy…so, I want to know what you two want from me or in general?" Cinco and Leslie looked at each other and then back to Jordan; Leslie cleared his throat and then nodded, as he sat forward on the couch. "Alright, I can damn sure answer that…I want you." Cinco shot Leslie a look and frowned; he then looked back at Jordan. "I'm your husband and I want you too, but I already got you, so what is this?"

Jordan blew smoke out his mouth and then sighed, as he looked between both guys. "I'm only saying this, because Cinco has been talking about having a threesome, with you Les…and you Les, just want me back. So, I'm serious about what I'm about to say now…" Both guys looked at each other and then back to Jordan, while in suspense about what he was about to say. Jordan nodded. "Me and Cinco are going to stay married, that's not going to change, but if everyone agrees, then Les can be brought into the relationship, as the third body and we all be in a relationship together." Both men stared at Jordan with their mouths open; he looked between both of them and frowned. "No one has anything to say?"

Cinco was taken aback, while Leslie was still confused; he frowned, before he spoke. "Wait a minute, so you want me to go back and be your sideline like I was before?" Jordan looked at him and then shook his head. "No…you'll move in with me and Cinco…me and him are married, so I can't marry you too; but I will treat you and Cinco as my husbands, equally." Cinco was still stuck on the first part and wasn't able to speak yet. Leslie raised an eyebrow and after it was explained to him, he didn't think that sounded too bad after all. Cinco looked at Leslie and then back to Jordan. "So, I'm not enough now? You need him with us to make you happy?"

Jordan sighed and then looked at Leslie. "Give me and Cinco a minute, Les…wait in the den." Leslie nodded; he stood from the couch and then walked out the living room.

Chapter 42

After Leslie walked out, Jordan got back to Cinco. "You are enough, but for some reason, you're having a hard time believing that. I love you and that's not going to change; you have the ring to prove that. You kept insisting we have a threesome with Les, but that's not going to work, baby. I don't know what you want any more either."

Cinco sighed and then rubbed his hands down his face; he then looked back at Jordan. "Jordan, I love you so much, and all I want is to make you happy, but I didn't think it would get this bad between us, where we needed an extra body in our marriage." Jordan shook his head. "It's not bad, Cinco; we don't have to do this…it was just a suggestion." Cinco nodded. "I only fucked him, because of the lies he was telling me; he made me think you didn't want me and was hung up on Tyler. Me and you weren't having sex either, so that made it worse and another reason I gave in." Jordan nodded and Cinco sighed. "I'm just curious how this would work...I mean, what exactly would happen?"

Jordan finished his cigarette and then put it out in the ashtray. "Well, I did think about this...so, he would move in with us and have his own bedroom, but he can sleep in the bed with us, if he wants or if I want. We continue our days the same, like me and you do now, with work and getting off from work; we all pay bills...and..." Cinco interjected. "What about sex? I mean, is it gonna be nonstop threesomes or something?" Jordan slightly laughed and then shook his head. "Not unless we all agree to do that...otherwise, I'll be having sex with both of you, whenever you two want it or I want it." Cinco slightly leaned his head to the side. "It sounds like you're trying to have your cake and eat it too." Jordan shook his head. "That's not it...no offense, Cinco, but if Les had a choice to be with me or you, then he's going to choose me. Do you want him, alone?"

Cinco sighed and then shook his head. "No...I told you what it was between me and Les and you're right about him not wanting me; if he was in the house, with us and had to choose, then I already know he's gonna wanna fuck you." Jordan sighed. Cinco turned his head to the side. "What about love? We both love you and you love me, so is there a chance you could love him again?" Jordan sighed. He didn't want to make the situation worse between him and Cinco, so couldn't bear to tell Cinco the truth...that he already loved Leslie and never stopped. Jordan knew he was in love with Leslie, but would never divulge that to Cinco or to Leslie, for that matter; at least not now.

Jordan cleared his throat and then slightly nodded his head. "Uh yeah, there is a great chance that could happen. I guess the ball is in your court now, because I don't want you to be uncomfortable or feel some type of way. If you think you're going to get jealous and continue to be jealous, then we're not doing it." Cinco slightly shook his head and thought this was crazy; he never heard of this before or been involved with something like this before. "Can you bring Leslie back in?" Jordan nodded and then got up to leave the living room; Cinco took a deep breath and shortly after, Leslie and Jordan walked back in. Leslie sat back down and Jordan did as well.

Cinco looked at Leslie. "Me and Jordan talked about it and we wanna try this with you; for a month first, to see how it goes. If I don't care for it, then we stop and you stay away from me and Jordan, for good." Leslie looked at Jordan and then back to Cinco. "Keep talking…" Cinco nodded. "I'm Jordan's husband, not you…you're gonna be his boyfriend; you move in with us and have your own bedroom, but Jordan said you can sleep in the bed with us, if you want or if he wants. Jordan pays the majority of the bills around here, but you still gotta financially contribute or compensate in other ways. I fuck Jordan whenever I want and you fuck him whenever you want…the threesome was my idea at first to make him happy, but I don't really want it; I'm good with it just being me and him alone. Me and you are not interested in fucking each other, but if Jordan wants to see us together, then we fuck, for him."

Jordan raised an eyebrow, as Cinco continued. "I know you love him but I love him too…so no dirty tricks, spying, lying, and nothing negative or that's your way of getting kicked out of this arrangement. No outside guys…if you agree to all this, then you belong to us, not nobody else; you cheat on Jordan, then your ass is out. I know it's gonna be hard, because it might be hard for me, but control your temper and keep the jealousy to yourself, if you got any."

Jordan stared at Cinco and then shook his head. "Damn, Cinco…I couldn't have said any of that better, myself." Cinco looked at him and then rolled his eyes, as Jordan slightly laughed. Leslie looked from Cinco and then to Jordan. "You're gonna have to put all that in writing, Jordan…I want a contract to protect myself, in case your husband tries to go back on his word." Jordan looked at Cinco and then back to Leslie. "Alright, I can do that…and uh, the three of us need to get checked; I want that with the contract too." The guys agreed and then Leslie stood from the couch; he looked between both of them and then sighed. "Ok, well I'll go get checked Monday, while y'all get this contract together; after that, I'll make arrangements on my end to get ready to move in." Jordan nodded and then Leslie said he was leaving.

After he was gone, Jordan looked at Cinco. "Are we really doing this?" Cinco looked back at Jordan. "Yeah, it looks like we are…trial basis for a month; put that in the contract." Jordan nodded and then smiled. "I love you…" Cinco got up and then went over to Jordan; he leaned down and then kissed him. Cinco pulled up from him and then smiled. "I love you too…"

Chapter 43

Three months later…

Jordan grabbed his mail and then walked in the house; he was combing through it, when he looked up and saw Leslie walking towards him. Leslie stopped at Jordan and then kissed him; he then pulled back from him. "Cinco is asleep…before you ask?" Jordan nodded. "Alright, well, it's Friday and…" Leslie interjected. "And your birthday, so…happy birthday, baby." Jordan rolled his eyes. "Don't remind me…" Jordan walked around Leslie and then made his way to the living room, with Leslie behind him. Afterwards, Jordan sat down on the couch and sighed, as Leslie went to the bar to make him a drink.

The arrangement between all three worked out great for the men; the first month trial, was perfect as far as Jordan was concerned. There were no issues and surprisingly to Cinco, Leslie was no longer angry and now tolerable; he respected the fact that Cinco was Jordan's husband and as long as he was labeled Jordan's boyfriend and not sideline, then Leslie was fine. All three men lived in the house together and Leslie had his own bedroom; he did share the king-size bed, in the master bedroom with Jordan and Cinco, almost every night. Jordan was having sex with both men and that arrangement worked out just fine as well. Cinco set his schedule at the club where he would be home on most nights to spend time with Jordan; Leslie still worked at the magazine with Arianna. The arrangement was a secret for now and no one knew about it, except the three men.

Leslie turned around from the bar and then walked over to the couch to give Jordan his drink; afterwards, he sat down next to him. "You act like you're turning sixty or something; you're still young, baby." Jordan took a sip of his drink and then shook his head. "This coming from the guy that just turned thirty a few months ago…so, for me thirty-six is close to sixty…" Leslie frowned and then laughed, as Jordan did too. "Anyway, it's just a few years older than me and one year older than Cinco, so don't act like you got twenty-five-year old's running around the house with you. You got plans tonight?" Jordan sighed and then shook his head. "No, but if I know my friends…and I do, then they're coming over here, if they don't hear from me." Leslie nodded. "It's time, Jordan…" Jordan looked at him and then frowned. "Time for what?" Leslie rolled his eyes and before he could speak, Cinco did. "Time to tell your friends about us…"

The guys looked at Cinco, as he walked in the living room. "Happy birthday, babe…" Cinco leaned in and gave Jordan a kiss, before walking over to the bar; Leslie looked back at Jordan. "He's right…Arianna thinks I calmed down at work, because I moved on from you." Cinco made a sarcastic sound. "She should know better than that." Leslie shot Cinco a look and Jordan laughed. Jordan swallowed down the remainder of his drink and then handed the glass to Leslie; he set it on the coffee table, as Cinco sat down on the other side of Jordan.

Jordan shrugged his shoulders and then looked between them. "Are you two ready to tell everyone?" Cinco looked at Jordan. "There's nothing for me to tell, I'm your husband and they know about me." Leslie rolled his eyes. "I'm ready…I been ready." Cinco shook his head. "I bet…" Leslie shot him a look and had words for Cinco. Jordan frowned and told both of them to shut up. "Do I need to send both of you to your rooms?" Cinco frowned, as Leslie sighed. Jordan shook his head and then looked at the time. "It doesn't even matter if I don't have plans tonight and if we're ready to tell or not…all of them are going to be ringing the damn doorbell soon."

Leslie sighed. "Look, Jordan…we're all happy and been making this work; I'm good and so is Cinco. We both make and keep you happy, baby, so might as well tell all of them what's going on." Cinco nodded; he was skeptical that this arrangement would work, but it has been and they were all happy. Both men did get jealous, as they knew they would, but didn't overreact and get angry.

Jordan rubbed his hands down his face and then sighed; he then looked between both of them. "Alright, well, I'm going to take a quick shower and put some different clothes on, and you two should just put some clothes on in general." Jordan stood from the couch, as the guys frowned. Both were in their boxer briefs. Leslie grinned. "You sure you want that?" Cinco rolled his eyes and then looked at Jordan. "We're about to change." Jordan shook his head and then walked out the living room; Cinco got up too and then went to change, but Leslie got up to see what they had to eat in the kitchen.

Chapter 44

Not too long after, the doorbell rang and Cinco slightly laughed, as he made his way to the front, while thinking about what Jordan said, about his friends. Cinco opened the door and then laughed. "Right on time, according to Jordan…he said y'all were gonna come over, if y'all didn't hear from him." Arianna made a sarcastic sound, as she walked in. "Well, he should have called then." Jorvik was right behind, along with Dimitri, Joron, Vance, and Trisha. Cinco closed the door after they were all in.

Everyone made their way to the living room and Arianna had a bag with her; she went to the bar, as Jorvik went to help her with the alcohol. Vance and Trisha sat down on the couch, next to each other, as Dimitri and Joron found a place to sit. Dimitri looked at Cinco, who was standing in the entryway of the living room. "Where is the birthday boy?" Cinco slightly laughed. "He's taking a shower and getting dressed; he said y'all were on the way." Vance nodded. "Uh huh, like Arianna said, he should have called if he didn't want us to show up; he knew better." Trisha laughed, as Joron joined her.

While everyone was talking and waiting for Jordan, Leslie walked up to Cinco, with his head down and a bowl in his hand; he started to speak. "Cinco, what the hell is in this bowl? I thought you cooked last night." Everyone frowned, as they stared at Leslie and saw that he was in his underwear. Cinco looked at Leslie and then cleared his throat. "Les..." Leslie frowned. "What?" Cinco turned back to everyone and Leslie followed his look; he saw everyone staring at him and then slightly smiled. "Hey, Arianna..." Cinco sighed, as Arianna frowned. "Hey, Les..." Cinco shook his head and then looked back at Leslie. "Jordan told you to put some damn clothes on." Leslie rolled his eyes. "I thought I had more time, but I was hungry...I wouldn't of came out here, if I knew what this poison in a bowl, was." Cinco frowned and both guys forgot that they had guests. "Poison? It's chili..." Leslie sarcastically laughed. "There's Wolf brand chili and Hormel chili, not Cinco chili...you can't cook worth a damn."

Dimitri had his mouth open, while Joron and Jorvik were confused as to what was going on. Cinco threw his hands up. "Well, you cook then..." Both men started to argue as everyone watched them. Jordan walked up to them and then frowned. "What the hell?" They stopped and Jordan looked at Leslie. "Are you going to get dressed?" Leslie rolled his eyes and then walked away from them. Jordan walked in the living room and then saw everyone staring at him. "Uh hey, everyone."

Vance raised an eyebrow. "Hey, Jordan…happy birthday." Joron laughed. Jordan looked at Cinco and then back to everyone, as he walked over to sit down. Cinco followed his lead and then did the same. Jorvik spoke. "What the hell is going on, Jordan?" Cinco looked at Jorvik and then back to Jordan. Jordan sighed and then shrugged his shoulders.

Arianna squinted her eyes and then a smile came across her face. "No fucking way…you did it, didn't you; all of you are doing it right now, aren't y'all? Unbelievable…" Joron frowned, because he was confused and Jordan slightly nodded his head. Vance slightly laughed. "Wow, I can't believe it." Dimitri interjected. "Only you Jordan, can pull off something like this…I mean, damn." Joron threw his hands up. "What the hell are y'all talking about? What did Jordan do?" Before Jordan could speak, Leslie did, when he walked in the living room, while eating ice cream. "He made me his man…" Leslie continued to eat the ice cream. Trisha raised an eyebrow and Vance laughed; Jorvik shook his head, as Joron frowned. "His man? What the fuck?" Joron looked at his brother, as Leslie sat down on the floor in front of the couch, where Cinco and Jordan were seated.

Jordan looked at Joron. "Calm down, Ron…Cinco is my husband and Les is my man; we all live here, together, and the majority of the nights, we all sleep in the same bed." Arianna hit her hand on the bar and Jorvik laughed. Joron had his mouth open, as Dimitri was still dumfounded. Vance shook his head. "Wow, just wow, Jordan…" Joron looked at Cinco. "You agreed to share your dude with another nigga? Y'all niggas are so sprung over Jordan." Arianna laughed, as Cinco rolled his eyes. Jordan looked at his brother. "Shut up, Ron…and mind your own business. How is my nephew doing?" Joron sucked his teeth and knew Jordan was trying to change the subject. "My little man is good, thanks for asking…Val at the house with Jaeda and the kids." Jordan nodded and was happy to hear that Joel was fine.

Dimitri looked at Jordan. "So, what are we doing tonight…hanging out here or going out?" Jordan looked at him and then shrugged his shoulders. "What do all of you want to do?" Joron looked at his brother. "You already know, I'm down for whatever." Vance frowned, as Jorvik slightly laughed. Cinco shook his head and then Leslie interjected, as he ate his ice cream. "I know this guy from when I did undercover work…he can get us in "Cobalt" if y'all wanna go: thirty and up spot." Arianna raised an eyebrow, as Jordan stared at Leslie.

Leslie looked up and then did a doubletake when he saw Jordan staring at him; he rolled his eyes. "The guy is straight…and don't know that I was flipped, on accident." Vance laughed, as Joron did too; Cinco frowned. "Flipped? Say, what?" Jordan cleared his throat and then looked at Cinco. "Les was semi-straight, when I met him." Cinco frowned, while Jorvik was outdone. "Damn, Jordan…I didn't know how far your powers went." Leslie laughed, as he ate his ice cream and Arianna shook her head.

Vance stood from the couch and then looked around at everyone. "Alright, well we're about to go home and get ready, so we'll meet all of you there tonight." Everyone else started to move around as well and shortly after, everyone was gone, except for Leslie, Cinco, and Jordan.

Jordan rubbed his hands down his face, as he stood from the couch; Leslie got up from the floor with his bowl and then looked between the guys. "I'ma go cut my hair and get ready." Jordan nodded and then Cinco looked at him. "You alright?" Jordan nodded. "Yeah, I'm fine. Come on, let's go get ready." Cinco nodded and then both walked out the living room.

Chapter 45

Everyone was at "Cobalt" and the club was packed; Jordan walked in with Cinco and Leslie. Dimitri was there already and with Jorvik, Joron, Arianna, Vance and Trisha. Arianna wanted to dance, so she and Jorvik went to the dance floor. Vance and Trisha went to a table, with the others. Dimitri sat down and then lit a cigarette, as Vance sat down; Trisha was about sit down, but said she had to use the restroom. Vance nodded and then watched her walk away. Jordan and the guys sat around the table and talked with Dimitri and Vance.

Trisha made her way through the crowd and was on her way to find the restroom, when someone stopped her; Trisha turned around and then saw Ryan. She slightly smiled. "Ryan…" He smiled and then nodded. "Hey, are you out with the girls tonight?" Trisha cleared her throat and then nodded. "Uh yes, something like that. What are you doing here?" Ryan sighed. "I'm out with friends…it's one of their birthdays." Trisha nodded and then slightly smiled. "That's good, well you have a good time." She was about to walk away, when Ryan grabbed her hand to stop her; she turned to look at him. "Come dance with me." Trisha frowned. "Right now?" Ryan nodded. "Your friends won't mind if you sneak away and have one dance with me." Trisha looked around and then back to Ryan; she nodded and he smiled. Both walked away together and then went to the dance floor. While on the dance floor, Trisha kept looking around, but then looked back at Ryan and hoped they didn't stay dancing for too long.

While this was going on, Valerie and Jaeda walked in together and had Daniel and his brother Eljay with them; Daniel had turned thirty-four during the week and asked Jaeda if she wanted to go out and celebrate with him and his brother. Jaeda accepted and asked Valerie if she wanted to go, so both accepted the invite. They all started to move to the music and then made their way to the bar to get a drink.

After they reached the bar, Eljay looked at the women. "So, what do y'all want?" Valerie shrugged her shoulders and didn't know, but Jaeda did. "Vodka shots." Valerie frowned, as Daniel slightly laughed; he nodded to his brother and then Eljay ordered vodka shots for all of them. Right after, they all received the shot glasses; Jaeda took hers and then quickly swallowed it down, as all of them watched her. Daniel raised an eyebrow. "Uh Jaeda, are you good?" She looked at Daniel and then nodded. "Hell yeah…" Eljay looked at his brother and then back to Jaeda. "You want another, or do you wanna go dance that off?"

Valerie laughed, as Jaeda smiled. "Three more shots and I'll be ready…" Daniel looked at his brother and then nodded again; Eljay ordered three more shots for Jaeda and after Valerie finished her first one, Jaeda was already almost done with all of her shots that Eljay ordered for her. Afterwards, Jaeda shook it off and then said she was ready to dance. Daniel told his brother that he and Jaeda were going to the dance floor; Eljay nodded and then after they left, Eljay and Valerie talked. It seemed that everyone was in a dancing and partying mood tonight.

Back at the table, Vance kept looking around and wondering where Trisha was, since she should have been back already. "Where the hell is Trisha?" Dimitri looked at him. "It's a club and she went to the restroom…you know how women's restrooms are." Vance nodded and decided to leave it alone. Cinco looked at Leslie and Jordan. "Y'all come on and let's go dance." Everyone looked at Cinco, and Jordan raised an eyebrow. "All of us…together?" Cinco nodded. "Yeah…" Jordan nodded and told Leslie to come with them; the guys left the table to go dance. Joron shook his head. "This shit, I gotta see." Vance laughed, as Dimitri shook his head.

They watched the guys go to the dance floor and then start to dance with each other. Vance shook his head. "Wow…" Dimitri frowned. "We should be recording this." Joron shot Dimitri a look and frowned. "For what? I don't even wanna watch no more." The guys laughed, as they watched Jordan in the middle, while Leslie danced in front of him and Cinco was behind him. Vance shook his head and looked away. "Jordan is acting like he's been living with two men his entire life." Joron laughed and then sipped his drink, as he looked out at everyone.

Chapter 46

As Jordan and the guys were dancing, they were spotted by someone. Terry frowned, when he saw Leslie dancing on Jordan, and then saw Cinco. Nick walked over to Terry with their drinks and then frowned when he saw the look on Terry's face. "What's wrong?" Terry looked at him and then back to where the guys were. "That's Jordan, right?" Nick got whiplash when he turned his head and then frowned, when he saw the sight. "What the hell…is he with Cinco and Leslie?" Terry pushed Nick out the way and then made his way to the dance floor; Nick set their drinks down and then followed Terry.

Terry and Nick made it over to the guys and then stopped. It was a slow song playing, so the guys were slow grinding on each other. Terry shook his head.

"What the fuck is this?" Jordan and the guys stopped dancing; they then looked to see Nick and Terry. Jordan looked between both of them, as if he didn't have a care in the world. "Nick…Terry…how have you two been?" Terry frowned, as he stared at Jordan; he then looked at Leslie. "So, you went back to Jordan?" Leslie rolled his eyes and then nodded. "Yeah, I went back to Jordan…" Nick shook his head and was confused. "I thought you and Cinco were married?" Jordan nodded. "We are…Cinco is my husband and Les is my man." Terry choked on his own spit, while Nick's jaw dropped. "What? What the…?" Cinco stopped his cousin. "Uh Nick, it's Jordan's birthday and we're trying to celebrate with him, so if you don't mind…"

Nick looked his cousin up and down. "Do what?" Terry dismissed everything said and got back to Jordan. "So, all this time…Les was really on your mind?" Terry then shot Nick a look. "I see you couldn't get the damn job done." Nick frowned, as he shot Terry a look. "Excuse me? He didn't mention Les not one damn time when I was with him." Cinco interjected. "And he hadn't mentioned you not one damn time, since he been with me." Nick shot his cousin a look and clenched his jaw. Leslie waved his hand around. "Terry, get the fuck away from us." Terry looked Leslie up and down with a frown on his face. "You're nothing but Jordan's bitch, Les…" Jordan clenched his jaw and then Leslie got behind Jordan, as the guys watched. Leslie held Jordan from behind and then kissed his neck, before looking back at Terry. "What's the matter, Terry…jealous?" Leslie looked at Cinco and then jerked his head over. Cinco stepped closer to them and

Nick frowned, as he watched Cinco kiss Jordan on the other side of his neck.

While this was taking place, Arianna and Jorvik stood there with their mouths open; they looked at each other and then back to the guys. Terry grit his teeth, as Jordan licked his lips. "Jealousy doesn't look good on either one of you." Nick started to stutter and then punched his cousin in the face; Cinco fell back and Terry laughed. Jordan looked at Terry and then punched him; the guys started to fight as Leslie joined in. Jorvik threw his hands up. "I fucking knew it!" He ran over, as Vance and the guys stood up from their chairs to see what was going on. Joron sucked his teeth. "Damn…" They all ran from the table and then made their way through the crowd, but on their way over, Vance turned his head and then did a doubletake. "What the fuck? Trisha!"

Trisha and Ryan both turned their heads, and Trisha put her hand over her face; Vance made a detour and went over to them. He looked between them and then Trisha spoke. "He asked me to dance and…" Vance interjected. "When…in the restroom?" Trisha tried to speak, but Vance didn't want to hear it; he grabbed her hand and attempted to pull her away, but Ryan interjected. "Hey, let her go." Vance looked him up and down. "Get the fuck out my face." Ryan frowned and Vance was once again about to walk away with Trisha, when Ryan once again stopped him. Vance had enough; he let go of Trisha's hand and then punched Ryan. Trisha moved back, as Ryan and Vance started to fight.

Joron was trying to help his brother in the brawl that he was part of, when he turned his head and frowned. "I know damn well…" Joron grabbed Dimitri and turned him. "Look…" Daniel and Jaeda had made their way through the crowd with Valerie and Eljay, to see what was going on. Dimitri started to stutter and then pushed Joron out his way; Jaeda saw Joron and then threw her hands up. "Oh, fuck…" Daniel rolled his eyes and no time was given before Joron ran over and slammed his fist into Daniel's face. Dimitri grabbed Valerie and aggressively turned her around to him. "What the fuck are you doing here and with him?" Valerie and Dimitri started to argue, as more fights broke out. Others became involved and the women got caught up in the fighting as well; Jaeda and another woman started to fight, when Jaeda was accidentally pushed by the woman. Arianna started to fight a woman that jumped on Jorvik's back; Trisha also started to fight a woman that was there with Ryan, and part of his gathering tonight.

The police were already called and while the fighting continued, many moved out the way or started to try to get away. Jordan was grabbed and put in handcuffs, as well as Nick, Terry, Leslie, Cinco, Arianna, Jorvik, Joron, Jaeda, Daniel, Eljay, Trisha, Vance, Ryan, Dimitri, and Valerie; all were arrested.

Chapter 47

Everyone was sitting in a holding cell and together; they were seated on the floor, or on a bench. Jordan shook his head, while sitting on the floor, with his leg up. Arianna looked at him. "Happy birthday, Jordan." Jordan shot her a look. "Thanks, Arianna…" Jordan looked around at everyone. "Well, since we're here…does anyone need an attorney?" Everyone looked at Jordan. Jaeda laughed, as Eljay and Cinco laughed too. Nick gave Jordan a snide look. "Why don't you shut up, Jordan?" Jordan frowned, as Cinco interjected. "Why don't you shut the hell up, Nick? This shit is your damn fault." Nick frowned. "Actually, it's Terry's fault." Terry looked at Nick. "If my memory serves me correctly, you threw the first damn punch, Nick." Nick shook his head. "Maybe if we didn't go over to them in the first place, then no punches would of been thrown. Over two years and you're still wondering if Jordan is thinking about Les?" Terry nodded his head. "Right Nick, and I guess Cinco and Les licking Jordan's neck on the dance floor, didn't really bother you." Arianna slightly laughed, as Joron frowned, as well as others.

Leslie sighed, as he looked at Terry. "Y'all shut the hell up…we were minding our own damn business, when y'all came over and interrupted us." Terry shot Leslie a look. "I'm sorry we interrupted you three dry fucking on the dance floor." Jordan rolled his eyes, as Cinco shook his head. Jaeda interjected. "Can y'all stop, y'all are making my head hurt." Joron frowned, as Eljay looked at her. "I think your head hurts from all the vodka shots you had, Jaeda." Daniel put his hand over his face and Valerie laughed to herself. Dimitri and Joron shot them a look.

Joron made a sarcastic sound. "So, you back fuckin' with this nigga, when I told you not to?" Jaeda and Daniel both looked at Joron; Jaeda sucked her teeth. "You said you didn't want me working at his barbecue spot, so I quit…you never said I couldn't hang out with him." Joron frowned. "What?" Cinco laughed, as Jordan looked down. Daniel sighed and then spoke. "We're all family, so what's the big deal if we hang out?" Joron shot Daniel a look. "Nigga, you ain't no damn family of mine…I'm not gonna tell you again to stay away from my bitch." Everyone shot him a look; Joron shook his head. "I mean, my wife…stay away from my wife." Arianna shook her head. "Nice save, Ron." Jorvik laughed, as others did too. Joron put his hand over his face, as Jaeda gave him a snide look.

"Yeah, that sounds about right, just say what you mean, Ron…" He looked at her and frowned.

Dimitri interjected. "You two had no business being out and with them." Valerie and Jaeda shot Dimitri a look; Valerie made a sarcastic sound. "Oh, really? Well, you went out with your friends, but I can't? I didn't know you put me back in sideline mode." Dimitri frowned and then looked at Vance; Vance looked back at him and then raised an eyebrow. "You're on your own with that one, Dimitri." Dimitri rolled his eyes and then put his hands up; he dropped them and then shook his head. "Fine, do what the fuck you want, Val…" Trisha threw her hands up. "We didn't do anything, but dance…me, Valerie, Jaeda…" Vance shot her a look. "Oh, that's all you did, huh? How about lying to me about going to the restroom and then sneaking off with that jackass." Ryan frowned. "Jackass? Well, this jackass was taking care of your wife and kids, after she left you." Trisha's jaw dropped, as Jordan raised an eyebrow.

Vance became enraged; he lunged off the bench and over to Ryan. Everyone got up from the floor, as Vance punched Ryan in the face; Ryan slammed Vance against the wall and then Vance put his hands around Ryan's throat. Jordan and Dimitri ran over to separate the guys, before someone came over and filed charges against them. Both were finally pulled back from each other. "Keep talking, bitch!" Jorvik threw his hands up and then shook his head, as he went to sit back down. Vance got loose from Jordan and then hit his fist into the wall; Jordan sighed and then everyone went back to their seats. Shortly after, three people walked over to the bars. Everyone turned their heads and Vance sighed.

213

Chapter 48

Randy shook his head with a grin on his face, while Lawrence and Lillian looked around at everyone. Lillian shook her head, as Vance rolled his eyes. "Well, when Randy called me, I couldn't believe that all of you were in jail, but now that I'm here and see who many of you are with, I understand now. Me and Lawrence are going to bail every last one of you out, but I have to have a therapy session with all of you first." Dimitri threw his hands up, as Arianna shook her head. Jordan sighed, as Ryan frowned. "I'm a therapist, so who are you?" Vance shot Ryan a look. "That is my mama, so say something else, so I can fuck the rest of your face up." Ryan rolled his eyes and kept quiet.

Lillian decided to start with Ryan, since he spoke first. "Ryan Graham…a therapist you say? An unethical therapist is what I would say." Everyone looked at him and Trisha sighed. Lillian sighed. "You had sex with your patient, while married…why did you really wait so long to inform Trisha, that you were married?" Jordan frowned, as Valerie raised an eyebrow. Ryan looked around at everyone and then to Trisha; he cleared his throat and then shrugged his shoulders. "I…I was in love with Trisha…still am, but it's not my fault. It's Vance's fault for treating her like shit their entire marriage. I tried to save her and my wife didn't understand how dedicated I was to my patients, to Trisha." Jorvik kept a frown on his face; Arianna frowned and Vance shook his head.

Lillian sarcastically laughed. "Your wife had an affair five years ago with your colleague; she bore a child with him, but you refused to give her a divorce at the time. Instead, you decided to mentally torture her…by flaunting your affair with Trisha in her face; you weren't trying to make her understand anything. You had an affair with Trisha, because she was vulnerable when she started seeing you. You took advantage of her and violated all your ethics by being involved with a patient. You may have finally divorced your wife, but you are still a snake. You are also a narcissist and after I report you to the medical board, you won't have to worry about falling in love with another patient again." Ryan choked on his own spit and Daniel raised an eyebrow. Jordan made a sarcastic sound. "Damn…" Vance slightly threw his hands up and then dropped them. "I don't know how you know everyone's business all the time." Valerie and Jaeda laughed, as Dimitri shook his head.

Lillian looked at her son. "Vance…Trisha loves you and all she did was dance, so move on, son…" Jordan laughed, as Vance frowned. Randy turned his head and laughed along with others. Vance rolled his eyes and then sighed, as Trisha looked at him. Lillian looked around and then spotted Dimitri; he saw her staring at him and then shook his head. "Please don't…can you just skip me?" Arianna and Joron laughed, as Lillian shook her head. "I can't do that, Dimitri…this won't take long…" Dimitri threw his hands up and then she continued. "You and Valerie are full time now and have been for a while; she was nervous about being full time with you, because she believed you were going to cheat on her. You did cheat and she forgave you…now it is in the back of your mind that when she is out of your sight, another man will take her from you. Not to mention that there is an age gap between you two…since you are thirty-six and Val is twenty-nine. You are more so worried as you become closer to forty, that a younger man is going to replace you." Leslie looked at Valerie. "You're twenty-nine? How did you get in the club, it's thirty and up?" Cinco shot Leslie a look and Jordan frowned. "The same way you got in." Jaeda laughed, as Eljay did too.

Vance put his hand over his face, as Daniel was in disbelief. Ryan sighed, as Arianna shook her head. Dimitri turned his head to the side and then back to Lillian. "As usual, Miss Brooks…always a pleasure." Jaeda shook her head and Valerie raised an eyebrow. "So, that's true, right?" Dimitri put his hand up to her. "Can we not talk about this right now?" Ryan made a sarcastic sound. "Why not? It looks like we're all gonna get our chance, so just shut up and take your turn." Vance frowned, as Arianna and Jorvik laughed. Valerie shook her head, as she stared at Dimitri. "Yeah, I resent you for putting me on a short leash, but I thought that was your ego, not you being insecure about your age and me leaving you." Dimitri crossed his arms, as she continued. "Dimitri, I love you and we have kids; I wanted to be your wife and I am, so that's it…and your age is not a problem for me. So, lighten up and trust me…me and Jaeda are friends and when I wanna come in town without you and the kids or however, then just trust me to come back home to you." Dimitri cleared his throat and then nodded. "I'm sorry, baby." Valerie nodded and then Lillian nodded too.

Chapter 49

Lillian looked at Jordan and smiled. "Mr. Ford…" Jordan smiled back at her. "Yes, ma'am…you are looking beautiful tonight, Miss Brooks." Arianna laughed; Vance frowned, and Dimitri rolled his eyes. Lillian shook her head. "You are such a charmer, Mr. Ford…and I haven't met anyone yet that doesn't love you." Nick made a sarcastic sound. "You got that right." Terry frowned, as some laughed.

Lillian sighed. "Actually, Mr. Ford, you and Arianna are doing just fine…even with your current situation; Cinco…Leslie…take care of Jordan." They looked at each other and then back to Lillian; both nodded. Dimitri frowned. "Wait a minute…Jordan has a husband and a boyfriend and he doesn't get scolded?" Trisha put her head down and laughed, as Vance and

Jordan did too. Lillian nodded. "Yes…Jordan played his cards well and surprisingly this situation that he is in, is perfect for him." Jordan shot Dimitri a look and then stuck his tongue out at him, like a kid. Dimitri rolled his eyes, as Arianna put her hand over her face and laughed; Jorvik shook his head.

Lillian looked between Nick and Terry. "Nick and Terry…" Nick threw his hands up. "Oh my God…" Lillian shook her head. "Nick and Terry, you two don't even want each other; both of you got together on the rebound from Jordan and Leslie, who are now involved in something that you won't ever understand. Terry, Leslie was never going to love you how he loves Jordan, so it was best that you two weren't together anymore. And you Nick, the scheming that Terry got you involved in, is probably what blew your chances with Jordan, in the first place. Regardless, it is done, over, and now the past. Both of you need to move on from Jordan and Leslie, as well as each other." Nick sighed, as he glanced at Jordan; Terry shook his head.

Lillian looked at Joron. "And last but not least…Joron and Jaeda. Once again, Daniel and Jaeda are just friends and Eljay is harmless too; they are Vance and Randy's stepbrothers. Yes, Daniel and Jaeda were intimate in Atlanta, but that was years ago." Jaeda sighed, as she looked at Daniel and he looked at her. Joron said nothing, as he sat there. Lillian continued. "Joron, Jaeda is your wife now and you also need to learn to trust her; she has your children and you've taken on the responsibility of a child that is not biologically yours, to make sure that he has a father. I know that when Jordan left you all those years ago, it broke your heart…he is your older brother and you blamed yourself for him leaving. He took care of you and your siblings and after he left, you felt abandoned; that he turned his back on all of you and left you with someone who didn't love you, as much as Jordan did." Joron slightly looked down, as Jorvik and Jordan looked at him.

Lillian continued. "It wasn't your fault and your efforts of trying to keep your children together and with you, made you manic. Jaeda is not going to take your children from you, not even Ju, even when you tried to take him from her. You can't change the past and treat your children like your siblings; your situation has changed and Jordan is not going anywhere. He is here and he loves you, so you don't have to worry about him leaving you again…or being separated from your children, like you and your siblings were."

Joron swallowed hard and then finally looked up; everyone looked at him and saw him staring out into space with tears coming from his eyes. Jorvik sighed, as Jordan got up and then went over to his baby brother; he hugged him, as Arianna sighed and Jaeda wiped her eyes. Jorvik went over to his brothers and hugged Joron after, Jordan did. Everyone was quiet and the therapy session had become very emotional.

Jordan looked at Joron. "Are you alright?" Joron looked at Jordan and then nodded, as Jordan spoke again. "I love you, Ron…ok; I love you, and I'm sorry." Jordan hugged his baby brother again, as Jorvik rubbed his hands down his face. Vance looked at Lillian. "Mama, I think you should wrap this up, now." Lillian nodded. "I just want to say one more thing to everyone…it is time to be happy and live." She looked at Lawrence. "You can get the officer now." Lawrence nodded and then walked away to get an officer; they had already made bail for everyone. Everyone stood up from the floor and bench to get ready to leave; their group therapy session was on everyone's minds.

Lawrence returned with an officer and then he unlocked the cell, to let everyone out. Nick cleared his throat, as he was about to pass Lillian. "Uh thank you, Miss Brooks." Lillian nodded at him and smiled; Terry thanked her too, on the way out. Everyone made sure to thank Lillian and Lawrence for bailing them out of jail and for the free session. The last to leave was Joron and Jaeda; he looked at her and then took her hand. "I'm sorry…" Jaeda nodded and then hugged him. "I love you…it's gonna be alright; we're gonna be alright." They pulled apart from each other and then Joron nodded; they walked out the cell and then left the police station.

Chapter 50

One month later…Thanksgiving

Lillian and Lawrence, who turned fifty-six, greeted their guests in the living room, as they arrived. Lillian hugged Valerie and Dimitri, and then smiled at the children, in which Dimitri had his daughter, Dimi with him for Thanksgiving; they had Mini and Dominic with them too. Lawrence shook the guys' hands. Jaeda and Joron walked in right after and Lillian hugged both of them, while Joron held the baby carrier with four-month-old Joel in it. Rydell and Giani were also there, with his son, eight-year-old Ry. Rydell was back in his wheelchair and Giani pushed him in; Lillian bent over to give him a hug. Ju said hi to Miss Brooks, as Jaeda held one-year old Jaelyn's hand. Lillian and Lawrence continued to stand together and greet their guests. Arianna, who turned thirty-one, and Jorvik were next with one-and-a-half-year-old Evan, as she held his hand; they were greeted, as well, as Jordan, Cinco, and Leslie. Vance and Trisha were last and Lillian smiled, as she looked at her son; she looked at her grandchildren and kissed them both. Lawrence shook Vance's hand. Randy, Daniel, and Eljay were already there.

All the kids were walking, even ten-month-old Dominica, or Mini; the only one that wasn't walking was Joel. Lillian had the food already prepared and ready to be eaten. Lawrence walked over to Lillian and then smiled. "Baby, the backyard is ready." Lillian nodded. "Ok, well, make sure everyone is comfortable; the boys like to watch the game, so is the projector set up?" Lawrence nodded. "Yes baby, everything is ready…the tables are set up, the servants are in place, food is out, canopies set up, seating, and the Disneyworld you had put in the backyard for the kids." Lillian slightly laughed and he did too. Lawrence smiled and then kissed her; it was a lingering kiss and the guys frowned. Vance shook his head. "Mama, please." Lillian and Lawrence pulled apart from each other and Lawrence rolled his eyes.

Lillian got everyone's attention and they looked at her. "Ok, everyone…the backyard is ready." Lillian turned around and everyone followed her outside. Once outside, Vance's jaw dropped and Trisha smiled. "Mama, this is too much…" Lillian frowned. "I want all my grandchildren to be comfortable and happy." Vance frowned. "All of what grandchildren, you only have two?" Lawrence cleared his throat, as he looked at Vance. "Uh Vance, your mama made us surrogate grandparents to everyone's children." Vance shook his head and Joron interjected. "Does that mean, we can drop them off over here?" Dimitri laughed, as Valerie and others followed his lead.

Everyone was in the backyard now with the kids. It was a nice day and the sun added a much-needed warmth to the cool air outside; Trisha took the kids over to the wonderland that Lillian had put in the backyard, for the children. It was a backyard that used to be plain with nothing in it, but ever since Lillian married Lawrence and everyone accepted her, she was happy and wanted to make her home more open, instead of the dark and cold home it was before.

Joron had set up Joel's portable playpen and had him under a canopy, with his blankets and a mosquito net, while he slept. Drinks were made, cigarettes were lit, and children were playing. Many had already sat down and made plates, while talking. Joron turned around from the playpen and almost bumped into Daniel; he sighed, as Daniel stared him. "Hey, uh I just wanna say I hope me and you are good." Daniel put his hand out and Joron looked at it; he looked back up at Daniel, as he slapped hands with him. For Jaeda, Joron was going to act as if he was alright with Daniel. "Yeah, man, we're good…but we'd be even better if you can find me a beer." Daniel laughed and Joron did too; the guys walked away from the playpen and then over to the other guys.

Arianna, Valerie, Trisha, Jaeda, and Giani were sitting together, while talking and eating. This was the first time that Arianna sat with the other wives and not with the guys. The women kept their eyes on the kids, but eleven-year-old Ju was the oldest and watching them, while Ry was with him. The guys were watching the game, as they ate and were yelling at the same time. Jordan got up and then went to make him another drink at the outside bar; he was making the drink, when Cinco and Leslie walked over to him.

Jordan turned around to them and he saw the look on their faces. Jordan rolled his eyes. "Don't tell me…Cinco you changed your mind about this arrangement and you Les, are tired of sharing." Leslie frowned, as Cinco sucked his teeth and then shook his head, no. "Everything is good, Jordan…we just wanted to tell you, that we love you." Jordan slightly squinted his eyes, as he looked between them. "And…? I know there's more or you two wouldn't be standing in front of me, together."

Cinco looked at Leslie and then back to Jordan; he nodded. "Yeah, there's more…Les told me, you like to watch." Jordan slightly frowned and then slightly laughed. "Ok…" Cinco nodded and then cleared his throat. "Well, tonight we're gonna do that for you…let you watch us." Jordan raised an eyebrow and then grinned. "Oh, really?" Leslie stepped closer to Jordan and then licked his lips. "Yeah, really…" Jordan eyed him and then Leslie kissed him; he pulled back from him and then Cinco stepped closer to him. Cinco also kissed Jordan; after he pulled back from him, Jordan slowly nodded his head. "Are you two, sure?" Both looked at each other and then back to Jordan; Leslie nodded. "We planned this for your birthday night, but getting arrested botched that." Jordan laughed and they did too.

Jordan nodded. "I love you both…" Cinco and Leslie nodded, as Jordan walked away from them with his drink; they watched him and then Leslie looked at Cinco. "I'm telling you now, Cinco, don't make me look bad in front of Jordan tonight." Cinco frowned. "What? I'm doing this for Jordan, not for you; if you look bad then that's on you." Leslie frowned and had words for Cinco, as they walked away from the table.

Lillian and Lawrence were together when Vance walked over to them; they turned their heads and Vance asked Lawrence if he could speak to his mama. Lawrence nodded and then walked away from them. After he was gone, Vance looked at his mama and then shook his head. "I don't know how you do any of the things you do or how you know so much about everyone, but if you didn't involve yourself in other people's lives, then none of us would be where we're at today. I love you, mama, and thank you, for ignoring my wishes of you staying out of my life." Lillian laughed and he did too; they stopped and then Lillian smiled. "All of you are me and Lawrence's family; there is no way around it…I never thought my life would be how it is now and I realized after I met Lawrence of how much of life that I missed and lost out on. I'm not alone anymore and isolated, but happy and free." Vance nodded and smiled. "That's great, mama…you deserve it. I'm going to get back to the game." She nodded and then Vance gave her a hug, before he walked away.

Afterwards, Lillian looked around and smiled at all the happy faces and laughing children. Lawrence walked back over to her and then put his arms around her from behind. "Are you alright, baby?" Lillian nodded. "Yes…happy that I wake up to you every morning." Lawrence grinned. "Same here…I love you." She turned around to him and then put her arms around him. "I love you too…how about we sneak in the house and…?" She stopped and he raised an eyebrow. "Right now, with everyone here?" She nodded and he didn't have to be told twice; he cleared his throat and then looked around, before taking her hand and then walking to the backdoor to go inside the house.

To be continued…

COMING SOON,

J WARE'S

6TH SERIES,

"TwinInsanity"

JAKLEENA 'J' WARE

Is an Independent author who currently lives in Spring, Texas, and has four children. She is a 2001 graduate of El Campo High School in El Campo, Texas. She received two Associates Degrees, in Occupational Studies for Auto Cad/Drafting and another in Applied Sciences for Paralegal. Her first series entitled, **Family Affairs**, has thirty-one volumes; her second series entitled, **The Toll Road Girls**, has twelve parts; her third series entitled, **Justified**, has twenty-eight parts; and her fourth series entitled, **Fontaine**, has thirty parts. All series are available on Amazon and Kindle. Her fifth series entitled, **Sidelines**, has seventeen parts. This is part thirteen of the seventeen-part series.